Clinton Ross

The Meddling Hussy

Being Fourteen Tales Retold

Clinton Ross

The Meddling Hussy
Being Fourteen Tales Retold

ISBN/EAN: 9783744661386

Printed in Europe, USA, Canada, Australia, Japan

Cover: Foto ©Andreas Hilbeck / pixelio.de

More available books at **www.hansebooks.com**

" 'There were three of us training that gun."

63

THE MEDDLING HUSSY

Being Fourteen Tales Retold

BY

CLINTON ROSS

NEW YORK
STONE AND KIMBALL
M DCCC XCVII

*THE author begs to acknowledge his in-
debtedness to the Messrs. Harper and
Brothers, the S. S. McClure Co., the Messrs.
Charles Scribner's Sons, the Batcheller Syn-
dicate, Mr. Bartlett Arkell of "Leslie's
Weekly," and to Mr. Lorillard Spencer of
the "Illustrated American," for permission to
reprint these tales. One, "The Extreme
Edge of Hazard," is reprinted through the
good favor of the Messrs. G. P. Putnam's
Sons.*

THE AUTHOR TO HIS READER

'TIS obvious that where there's a story there's a woman. Though Louis Stevenson often was pleased to ignore her, still she was somewhere in the experience of his characters. So I have ventured to call this collection by one of the tales, " The Meddling Hussy ; " not indeed because I hold that tale of better quality than the others, nor because a woman appears in them all, — but because she is ever a-meddling with our affairs, and, for the most, improving them and making them endurable.

You will notice, should you be induced to read them all, that there are included tales of American wars, and two others which are historical, and three which are the slightest comedies of the New Road, and one a tale of a ship's smoking-room. You may ask why

subjects so divergent appear under one cover;
and I will say that the sole reason is that
the author is trying to prove his case. Ah,
how difficult is that proof, dear Reader! I
call you dear Reader, trusting that the kindly
person, who presided over English letters a
century since, may have a descendant.

I am then,

Yours faithfully,

CLINTON ROSS.

At New York,
4th Oct., 1896.

Contents

Part I

Tales of American Wars

Part II

Tales of Personages

xi

Contents

Part III

Tales of the New Road

Part IV

A Tale of an India Mystery

A Tale of the Ghost of the Stretching Moor

Part I
Tales of American Wars

The Confession of Colonel Sylvester

The Confession of Colonel Sylvester

SHE stood against the doorway of the manor house as I rode up, and she was handing her bridle-rein to a fat Dutch boy. If her faded green habit told of sun and rain, it told no more than the thin, flushed face and the eyes that questioned my approach. I fidgeted, thinking of woman's tears, dismounted as clumsily as a boy who is learning the saddle, bowed as awkwardly as any lout. Yet I might not have been so troubled, I 'll confess it, had she been old and ugly.

Not that she was reckoned, by standard of feature, attractive; but there was something piquant in the turn of her nose, and in the moulding of her lips, which seemed to hold either laughter or severity.

Confession of Colonel Sylvester

" I wish to see Colonel Van Brule, if I may ? "

I thought she paled.

" He is not at home, sir. Who shall I say ? "

" John Sylvester. May I not wait for him ? "

" He will not be back to-day. What do you want ? "

The question was direct, and, I dare say, I should have used subterfuge, but something in her eyes forbade. I did not like my mission at all, under their scrutiny.

" I came to take him to General Washington."

" Mr. Washington wishes my father ? "

" General Wash — "

" Ah, I forgot, sir. You are a rebel officer. But we can't address a person who has not the king's permit by a title other than the common one."

" It does n't matter about titles, Miss Van Brule, but facts, you know. I believe

Lord Howe had a little dispute about them, and ended by calling the general, General Washington." I was piqued by her contemptuousness.

"His Lordship has need to be politic. Yet, although we are on different sides of the question, Mr. Sylvester, I'll try to be hospitable, remembering you have had twenty miles in the saddle. If you'll come in, I shall be glad to offer you tea."

"I shall be glad, but — "

"I had forgotten a rebel would sooner drink poison," and she laughed softly in my face.

"You see," said I, fidgeting, "I really came here to arrest Colonel Van Brule, and your invitation is such a coal of fire — "

"Oh, is it? I only thought it simple good manners, but if you want — "

"Oh, I will — gladly — if you will excuse my embarrassment. Really this mission was not to my mind. I am sure

Confession of Colonel Sylvester

General Washington intends only to detain Colonel Van Brule for a few hours, and — "

But she did not appear interested.

" And now, sir, if you 'll do us the honor."

She went before, turning around with a curious expression that I could not explain. Was she trying to give Colonel Van Brule chance to escape? I had seen no one except her and the boy. The hall, extending the length of the house, the square room into which I was ushered, both were deserted; and here, with a smile, a little bow, she left me.

I stepped to a deep-set window, the thick shutters fixed with heavy iron bars, looking out over the green slopes to the Sound. Some men were harvesting — a strange sight when all about was war, and rumor of war. An opening door led me to turn about, when I saw a courtesying serving-woman, who laid out a service of tea and cakes. The silver bore the Dutch arms; the china was some rare sort; and just then the door opened on the mistress of the manor, who had changed her gown to one that might not have been misplaced in town. She said something to the woman, who went out.

"Will you have tea? The fact is, my father and I are the only members of our family, and, now, the times being so disturbed we do little visiting. Let me see — I have been nowhere for a week, when I was a day at the Philipses."

"Really this is the most delightful hospitality."

"Particularly because unexpected," she said, with a curious expression in that well-toned voice. "Oh, I 'm a poor player. This is false hospitality — for — I have you here as prisoner."

"A prisoner," said I, looking at this undeniably handsome lady of the manor, and wondering if she might be mad.

"Yes, prisoner. I really am sorry to say it, but it 's necessary — "

"And why?" And then recovering myself, with a weak attempt at gallantry, "I'm not an unwilling one, I'm sure."

"You don't care to be in the battle which will be on Long Island to-morrow?"

"A battle?"

"Oh, yes, a battle; and it was necessary for me to detain you here, because my father has gone to Long Island, and I did n't want you to know it, as you would if you left here."

"But I can go, can't I?" said I, as if she were jesting.

"A man with a musket is behind each door."

"And my men?"

"Are disarmed, and guarded in our stable. You would better sit down," said my hostess, demurely. And then I noticed by her plate a little pistol. Seeing my glance, she said, flushing:—

"And I know how to use a pistol. I do not rely entirely on my men."

Confession of Colonel Sylvester

" Yes, frankly," said I, collecting my wit, " I have my sword and pistol. You have your pistol, your charming self, and some Tory servants — "

" About twenty, Mr. Sylvester," she said, looking me over.

" But why should my knowledge of Colonel Van Brule having gone to Long Island be dangerous ? "

She hesitated; and I saw that although she knew it was more discreet not to tell, a common feminine weakness — a wish to flaunt her triumph — led her to the fact.

" I don't know why I should n't tell. My father is this moment showing Sir Henry Clinton an unguarded pass among the Bedford Hills. By occupying it, the king's troops will be able to turn the rebel flank — is that the right term ? "

I did not apologize for what I said.

" Please to sit down. We will dine directly. Don't go to that door. I 'm in earnest in saying I have a man stationed there with orders to shoot you down if you try to go."

" But why should I be detained ? How could I have had the information — which you give me yourself ? "

" I was afraid you might find out from some spy, and stop my father before he could reach Long Island."

" But why do you tell me about what he intends ? " I still questioned.

" I suppose to justify my false hospitality. I really don't like what I 'm doing."

" It 's very extraordinary of — a woman."

" Oh, is it ? But all 's fair in war."

" Love and war," said I, reflecting ; and at twenty-five one does n't like to show too much chagrin before a pretty woman.

" The poets are silly. There 's a lot that 's unfair in both."

" Yes ; I think this is unfair," said I, trying to appeal to her sympathies.

I must outwit this little intriguer. I must get word to New York. If there were to be a fight, I too must be in it. And it was certain that we stood every chance of being surrounded, should Sir Henry get behind General Putnam, should the ships of line beat up the bay.

My hostess had been noting me, and, I think, reading my thoughts.

" I 'll speak to Gretchen about bringing the dinner in here — instead of the dining-room."

" Why here ? "

" I can guard this room more conveniently. Will you excuse me ? "

I noticed she held the little pistol close. As the door shut I heard a key turn on the outside. Quickly I walked to the window out of which I had looked; and then I heard her voice.

" Really, Mr. Sylvester, it is only fair to warn you that if you get out that window you 'll be shot down."

'T was a shot from her eyes I had, debating the chances of running and warning my chief of the plot I had found in this Westchester manor. But I did not see very clearly how I should; for I had not doubted she spoke truly, and that I was too well guarded to have any chance left. She stood in the room now, looking me over with triumph, her hands crossed behind her.

" I confess, Miss Van Brule, I am your prisoner," after waiting for her to break the silence.

" Apparently," said she, with a suspicion of a smile.

" If all the Tories are like you, I suppose we may as well give up now as any other time."

" Oh, your case is hopeless. Frankly, I 'm sorry for you. But how can a man of your position take up with the wrong side ? "

" My personal opinion — that is all. My brother is as decided for the king as you."

" I suppose if you once had taken my father to New York, he would have been thrown into prison like Major Matthews."

"I think he was called to New York simply that he might be questioned."

"And by what right would they question him, who is responsible only to the king's government?"

But how could I answer a question of opinion on which the whole dispute hung?

"Your mission was contemptible. If I may have played you a trick, I'm not ashamed of it. I am only sorry I thought proper to apologize."

She said this spiritedly, eyes flashing, face reddening.

"Oh, I don't blame you, Miss Van Brule."

"Do you think I care whether you may or not?"

"That's the trouble," said I, "you don't. I wish you did."

"And then you might have a chance to get out of this fix," said she, smiling.

The same old woman, as the afternoon

paled, came in, removing the tea-table, and making ready the dinner. I did not see the evidence of any one at all in the hall when I peered into its recesses.

"Oh, you need not look, Mr. Sylvester. Your guard is not far away?"

"But if I took the chance?"

"I should hate to have you shot." I fancied the serving-woman smiled.

"I don't exactly fancy it myself, being rather fond of life, you know."

"You should not be too serious. You forget it's unbecoming at dinner," said she, lightly, passing the bread.

"You must pardon my poor manners —under the circumstances."

"They must be put to rather a test," looking at the little pistol beside her plate.

"Now suppose I should snatch that?" I began.

She snatched it herself, trembling, and reddening, as she had a way of doing, I had found.

"But you would n't, Mr. Sylvester."

"And why not? Because it would be ungallant? I easily could take it, and frighten you into letting me go."

"Yes, you might; but I have been warned."

"Oh, I will not. Put your pistol away, Miss Van Brule."

"Really; on your word of honor?"

"I have said I would n't."

"Well, then, I will put it there by the plate."

"Thank you. I have to thank you for much — first an invitation to tea — and then dinner."

"And imprisonment."

"A delightful one — on account of the gaoler."

"Oh, you are very gallant. I dare say you have had practice enough."

"Now I have provocation."

"If you don't mind, I have small taste for pretty speeches."

"I can't help them."

"Possibly not. But, to change the subject, I am bound to amuse you in some way. What do you say to chess ? "

I played an indifferent game, I told her, when she took out the board, and the servant began to clear the table. Candles were brought, and we sat down, she having the first move. Watching her, I easily was checkmated, and of course asked for revenge, saying it was only fair, seeing she had checkmated me, not alone in chess. And so we sat there in the old house, I the prisoner, and she the gaoler, moving our pieces, while down in the city, and on Long Island, the game of war was playing. Suddenly she grew distraught, making some mismoves, out of keeping with her skill.

" You have lost your queen."

" Oh, I can't play," she cried, bursting into tears. " I hate it."

A woman in tears, I don't know what to say and do ; and now I made the most clumsy attempts, apologizing for what I knew not, and asking what I could do ; and she laughed, but said gravely, —

" I was thinking of my father over there on Long Island. He may be in danger — he is."

" But the game. I shall checkmate you this time."

" No, you won't, because I won't play."

" Now that 's truly feminine."

" Yes, it is — to give in because I know I 'm beaten."

" I suppose that is the case."

" Oh, I see you know women."

" Well, I 'm not so sure."

" Oh, I thought you were."

" Oh, I beg your pardon. The young lady who takes a prisoner of war certainly perplexes one a bit."

"Does she ? Ah, does she ? "

And she changed the subject.

The clock, somewhere in the hall, sent out a sepulchral ten.

" Jacob will show you your room."

" My dungeon, I suppose."

" Oh, well, our houses may not be so

comfortable as those in Maryland. Jacob!"

"Yes, 'um." The boy seemed to have been in hearing, and now was in the door-way, round, fat, curious.

"I believe your parole does n't extend to trying to get away?"

"Only to seizing your pistol, and turning into an escaped prisoner."

"There's one window in your room, but a man will watch under it."

"Oh, I dare say."

"It's a pity you 're on the wrong side."

"It's a pity you are, if you will allow me."

"You are incorrigible. Good-night."

"Good-night," said I, extending my hand. "I have had a delightful evening."

"It's quite as if you were only my guest."

"Quite." I could not resist pressing the hand, when she withdrew it angrily.

"By the way, I hope my men are comfortable?"

"They have every attention under the circumstances."

"So it appears, have I?"

She did not answer this sally, and I followed Jacob into the hall, and upstairs.

"When would you like to have me bring your shaving-water?" said Jacob.

"But I have n't razors."

"I 'll fetch Colonel Van Brule's, sir."

He took the shilling with a grin, showing his teeth like a Maryland darky. But I could not prevail on him to tell me about the force of the manor. He locked the door behind him, and I saw it was heavy oak, and could not be broken in easily. It was very dark, but I thought I could see a figure under my window on the lawn.

And, then, I sat down to think over the extraordinary adventure.

Here I was caged by a girl, as many a man before, and since, has been; and I knew — because I could not deceive myself — that I doubtless had not tried to get away as I might have if this young lady had been, say, Colonel Van Brule. I could not make out why she should detain me, unless indeed it had been all as she had said, and the colonel really was show-ing the pass in the Bedford Hills. Would she let me go in the morning when the mischief was all done; or turn me over to the British? She really was quite capable of it. At any rate she was an extraordi-nary young woman. I fancied she was opposite me at the chess-board. We were playing a most exciting game for some stake that I held dear, and I always was check-mated; and always was that smile from the enigmatical gray eyes. And in my bad temper I overturned the board, when the low boom of guns broke in on the stillness — probably the men of the manor, carrying out their mistress's orders.

I was rubbing my eyes. The August dawn was contending with burnt and sput-tering candles. But if I had been dream-ing all night there in the chair, the rumble was distant, yet unmistakably that of heavy guns. The wind was in the right direction; and I knew that the fighting at last had begun on Long Island. But how was it going? Was the position indeed surrounded? Was the fleet shelling the town?

Asking these questions, I was now looking out of the window, where the darkish dawn was scattering the shadows from the hollows of the hills. If I had fancied I had seen a figure guarding, there was no one now in view. Opening the window, I measured the distance, some thirty feet, debating whether I should try it. Should I, it doubtless would be with the consequence of a broken arm or leg, and that only would hinder my chance of escaping. If I could not help the situation by giving the warning, I, at least, wanted to be in this fight. I had been in none yet, and at twenty-five I longed for it, wondering whether, like Frederick of Prussia, I should run. All the drilling we had done with

Smallwood's, all our talk over what we should do, returned with an insistence for action on my part. I tried the door and saw again I was not equal to breaking it in. And again looking out of the window, I threw myself on the bed, while a plan began to formulate which was connected with Jacob and the shaving.

And while I considered, and the hours passed, the far-away guns kept up a dull chorus.

But finally, as I had expected, came the knock, and Jacob's voice; and when I answered the creaking key, and Jacob with the shaving-water, and a civil "good-morning, sir," I asked him to put the pitcher on the table, and then, as his back was turned, I was on him, holding his arms, with a hand over his mouth, and bearing him to the floor. Strong as he was, I was wiry, and had the advantage. We must have made a fearful noise in the house, overturning chairs and the table. Every moment I expected interruption, but kept on, choking the poor Dutch boy just enough so that he gasped, giving me a chance to tear the sheets from the bed, and to bind and gag him. He stared in a pathetic way; felt keenly, I knew, his duty to his mistress. But I had no time, and taking my sword went hastily into the hall, and there half way on the stairs she met me. No one else was in sight, and, suddenly, something occurred that made my position ridiculous. What if from the first she had been tricking me? What if there were only she, the woman, and the boy in the house? And I had submitted as easily as you could wish.

"Where are the others?" said I, pausing at the head of the stairs, sword in hand against this girl.

"I — I don't — " she began in confusion, and I saw she was haggard in the morning light.

"You fooled me, Miss Van Brule. There were none."

"Two men in the stable, while I certainly should have shot you myself if you had tried to get away."

" You 're cleverer at this game than at chess. And I believed you —"

" Yes, you did."

" And you, doubtless, intended delivering me to the British?"

" Frankly, I did."

" Oh, I 've been prettily deceived —"

And I pushed past her.

" What did you do with Jacob?"

" I killed him," said I, wickedly.

" You wretch! You dared?"

There were tears in the gray eyes, and in an instant I had added, —

" Oh, I did n't at all. That firing made me desperate —"

" And me. My father may be in it."

" And I will be."

At this moment I heard heavy steps, and suspecting I might be caught after all, I dashed down the stairs, almost knocking down a fellow with a musket. And then I heard her voice, —

" For Heaven's sake don't fire. Let him go."

That was odd, was n't it? But I did not pause to think about it, but ran out through the door, and down the slope to the road, and over the fence. I must have made a strange appearance in the scarlet and buff of Smallwood's, with a drawn sword in my hand, running there in the Westchester fields. (When I had joined the general's staff I still kept my Maryland uniform.)

And then I paused, and fell to laughter over the joke. What a silly fool! This girl had turned me about her finger. An adroit tactician, indeed, I! But folly usually is culpable. By my blindness I had failed to give the warning that might now be turning the day against us over there on the Island. My pretty Tory had tricked me neatly.

I had forgotten my men; and I turned back. The trickery should n't extend that far.

Confession of Colonel Sylvester

I walked boldly now to the stable door, no one hindering. A big fellow was currying a horse.

" My men, rascal ! "

He stood in open-mouthed wonder and fear, for I must have appeared vicious.

A pounding on an inner door here began, and the cries of my two fellows, one of them declaring that the door would n't break. He had been trying it all night, with his strength.

" Open," said I, threatening the groom with my sword. He decided to open, growling his remonstrance. My two would have killed him then and there, until I had to swear at them — a thing I 'm loath to do at one's inferiors ; but sometimes it is necessary. They were hungry and sad-looking crows ; for although they had been driven into the little dark harness-room at the butt of the musket, their captors had not dared to go near them. I told them to get the horses ; and then, better satisfied with myself, I sauntered up to the house.

She stood before the door, looking at me defiantly.

"Good-day to you, Miss Van Brule."

She tossed her head disdainfully.

"The game is my way."

"Why should n't it be? You 're a man."

"I regret I must exact reparation."

"What do you mean?"

"I must take you to New York as a dangerous Tory."

Her eyes flashed, and she stamped her foot.

"It's like you rebels — to make war on women."

"You started it."

"Ah, I did keep you here," she cried; "and Sir Henry has them surrendered, I know."

I called to my men to bring up my horse. They were still murmuring over their treatment, and eyed the mistress of the manor malevolently. But I stared at them, and told them to ride on, which they did grumblingly.

" Good-by," said I to her.

She looked me full in the face.

" But I 'm sorry — to have tricked you — really — "

Have I not said my pulse was easily made riotous ?

" Don't be," said I.

" You 're silly," said she. " And — "

" And what ? "

" We don't know each other — and you 're rebel."

" That means you always will hate me ? "

" Oh, I did n't say that. Why don't you go on after the men ? "

" I will — when you tell me to call again."

" Oh, do, if you only go."

There was that in her eyes telling more.

" How dare you ? " said she.

Confession of Colonel Sylvester

As I rode away, I looked back at the little trickster of the manor, who stood blushing as I had left her, and I doffed my hat, and called back, "We shall meet again;" and we did, as you know. But that morning, with the dull boom of the guns from the battle at Brooklyn in my ears, I whipped up after my men on my tardy way to the war.

The Colors of the " Lawrence "

The Colors of the " Lawrence "

A Surgeon's Tale of the Lake Battle for the West

MASTER Commandant Perry stood talking with Master Commandant Eliot of the " Niagara." Captain Perry's eyes — I will call him captain, although he had not that title then — moved uneasily. For the moment I thought him too young. What could he do against the one-armed veteran of Trafalgar, Captain Heriot Barclay? Lieutenant Buchan, too, had fought with Nelson. Thump went my heart as I leaned over the rail, and Sailing-Master Taylor, brushing against me, rallied me on my pallor.

" Humph, doctor, are ye ready? "

" We 've orders to have our instruments bared in that cock-pit," said I.

47

The Colors of the " Lawrence "

" It 's a cock-pit too high up, eh ? " said the sailing-master; and I assure you he was right about the wretched hole.

" What will ye have when a twenty-four-pounder comes sailing through the new oak and chestnut ? "

I shook my head. He chuckled and passed on. I saw a great bird sailing high above, and the stretch of lake, — saw, and did not see; for I was thinking just then of a girl I knew in New York, and of how I should have liked to see her for a moment. And then I was reminded by a groan below of a poor chap in the delirium of lake fever. And as I looked out at the ships lined before me, it all returned: the journey to Albany, and down the Mohawk, and over the corduroy roads, and on the lake in the dreary March winds, and the lonely sail to Presque Isle, and the dismal life we led at the tavern flaunting the creaking sign " Dunlop's Erie Hotel."

From the first it had been a perilous journey, an uncertain enterprise. No one supposed we could hold the West. Any moment the enemy's fleet might sweep down on us, and our captain, short of men, must have lost heart writing letters for supplies, — imploring them to send shipwrights, sailors, and money.

And now we were to fight! There the white fleet lay on the rippling lake over against us. Nine vessels were in our line, we of the " Lawrence " first. Yet these schooners and sloops were manned by as sorry a lot as captain ever had shuddered at. But a hundred and twenty-five were regulars; and the rest were raw enough, — woodsmen, negroes, and Indians, who knew no more of a ship than squalling babes. And, indeed, that moment Pohig, a Narragansett brave, said in his guttural they needed me in the cock-pit. I think I said something uncomplimentary to that cock-pit, which was already over-crowded, for there were twenty-two under doctor's care on the " Lawrence " alone, and indeed a hundred and sixteen

unfit out of the four hundred and ninety
of the fleet.

I paused a moment, looking out again
at the beauty a sunny September morning
gathers in these waters. The six white
ships of the king still bore on, with flaunting canvas, carrying all told, as I was to
know later, five hundred and two souls :
one hundred and fifty from the Royal
Navy, while of the two hundred and forty
soldiers most were regulars. From that
fleet I turned to ours. I had forgot my
summons to the delirious chap below. I
should have something besides mere fever
to deal with before that day was over.
And then among our motley crew I saw
some men who had been on the " Constitution." Ah, they stood straight and fine,
with just the right swing. Some of our
fellows, after all, were not so bad.

At the moment a blue flag was unfurled
at the main royal masthead, declaring, in
white letters, " Don't give up the ship."

I watched the men curiously, and before I thought joined in the cheer. I had not heard in my reverie that the captain had been saying : " Shall I hoist it ? " nor the answer, " Ay, ay, sir ! " But now that it flew in the breeze it declared Captain Lawrence's last words, and swung out over the hastily built lake brig which the Secretary had given that bravest captain's name. Then was the beating to quarters ; and I remembered my summons to the cock-pit.

A little fellow — once rosy cheeked, but now shaking with the ague — had asked for me.

" Don't tell me, doctor, that I can't be in it."

" Look here, Fraser," I said, " be quiet. You can't stir, do you hear ? " I was irritable ; but, remembering my professional manner, I added, " Oh, we 'll see."

" The captain wishes you in his cabin, Mr. Moran," some one interrupted. I pressed Fraser's hand, and joined the captain. He was tying some papers, and turned to face me with a smile.

"The government's papers, Moran," he said. "We'll have a pretty warm time, I fancy, and you'll be busy."

"I dare say, — busy," said I.

"I hope not too busy, Moran. But you are the safest man to keep this packet. Should it go against us, — I have tied some shot to it, — drop it into the lake."

"Ay, ay, sir," said I, taking the papers. "How are you feeling?"

"I don't seem to be over that trouble," he said, tearing up some letters.

"You certainly are not," said I, looking him over narrowly.

"What luck, when I need all my nerve!"

"You will have it, sir," said I, pouring something from a vial, for I had brought my case.

As he drank, he scattered the bits of torn paper — "My wife's letters," — which made me think of the girl in New York, whom I had reason to believe might be thinking of me. Should I ever see her again?

" I don't care to have them get my private correspondence. As for the other papers — "

" I 'll have that care."

" Pardon me, I know you will, Mr. Moran. But you see I 'm nervous."

" I don't wonder."

" No, it means so much. The people don't realize that if we lose to-day they will carry out the old French idea, and Canada will reach clear to the gulf."

" And the United States will stop at Ohio forever after," I added. " But they have n't done it."

He seized my hand at this. " No, they have n't." His eyes sparkled. " After all we have been through, and made and floated the fleet, it makes one fearful when the moment comes."

" Yes, it is here, sir. Listen."

It was a bugle call, followed directly by " Rule Britannia."

The Colors of the " Lawrence "

" That 's from the ' Detroit.' "

" Their flagship."

" We are getting near. Hear the answer to ' Rule Britannia.' "

It was just our boatswain's whistle, but a faint color crept over his face; and then seizing my hand, he went above, calling back, " My work now, and yours, will begin," which took me again to the cock-pit. As I moved about, putting the last touches to the place, I heard that grog and rations had been served, because we doubtless should not have the chance later. " He says we know how to beat those fellows," said one, a petty officer who was among those from the " Constitution." " Why, we 've done it. We 'll do it again."

" What are you doing now ? " said I, turning.

" I heard the captain say to Mr. Taylor, ' Run to the lee of the islands; ' and Mr. Taylor says, says he, ' Then you 'll have to engage to leeward.' ' I don't care,' says our captain; ' windward or leeward, they 'll have to fight to-day.' Eh, doctor, he 's the captain."

" I believe he is, Perkins," said I; then Perkins chuckled, hitched his trousers, and went above. But directly I heard that a shift had put us to the windward.

And then the first gun broke in on the rattling noises of our deck, and others answered.

I rushed above, and watched the men at their posts, bared to the waists, muscles standing out tensely, faces set or twitching. A burst of smoke already was blurring that clear sky. And then something crashed into our deck, and the splinters flew as the report rang loud in my ears. I believe I just looked about coolly at our line, the schooners and sloops drawn up, a half-cable's length of each other. Lieutenant Yarnell observed me and nodded.

" The ' Lawrence ' is to have most of this battle," he said. " The ' Queen Charlotte ' is training on us."

The Colors of the " Lawrence "

He scarcely had spoken before we heard a great crash above, and our mainmast tottered. The sound was followed by another rush of breaking timbers, and some one was shouting there was a hole in our hull. I did not notice now. I was watching two groaning fellows who were being carried below ; and I hastened to the work there. These were hardly stretched out before others were brought. Their suffering faces stare at me even now of nights ; and in dreams I can hear their cries in a deafening din.

And I, too, was stripped to the waist, turning now and then to inquire. We had drawn to closer quarters, and were engaging the " Detroit," the " Queen Charlotte," the " Lady Prevost."

" I believe I 'm done for," said a groaning fellow, and I saw it was my friend Perkins, the petty officer.

" Nonsense," said I, turning him on his side.

" I 'm not groaning at that hole, doc-

tor," said he, " but because the cannon-
ading has made it fall calm, and the others
can't support us.   Oh, but it does hurt."

" It's only a scratch," said I.   " But
the ' Scorpion ' and the ' Ariel ' are close
behind us."

" They alone, and engaging the ' Chip-
pewa.'   It looks bad, doctor."

" Oh, ' don't give up the ship,' " said I.

" That we won't," he cried, pushing
me aside.

" Come back, man," I cried.

" I'm bandaged enough," said he, and
was gone.   The next I saw of him was
when an hour later I stumbled over his
body.   I should have hindered his return
to his post ; but I had no time to follow
him, for others were being brought con-
stantly, until we knew not where to put
them, much less to give them proper care.
My arms absolutely dripped with blood
and perspiration, and those we tended
were black and red with powder and
worse.   A crash in the china closet was

followed by a howl, and I remembered Midshipman Forest had left his spaniel there.

" We 're all howling," I muttered, half crazy myself.

" Dress that, doctor," came a faint voice over my shoulder.

" Presently," I said ; then I saw he was Midshipman Lamb.

" Let me see," I believe I said, when there was another horrid crunching of timbers, and Lamb was against the side, where he had been carried by a twenty-four-pounder. I rubbed my eyes, and at that moment another of these tearing pounders sailed past my assistant, Usher's head.

You can imagine we could do nothing in such a place ; that we lost the little wit we had, although I tried as well as I might. Twice Lieutenant Yarnell came below, pointed to his arm or face, and, when we had tied him up, went back to his post.

" How is the captain ? " I asked.

" A shot through his hat, and his clothes all torn, but I don't believe he 's hurt."

" You 're not fit to go above."

" Where can you stow me ? " he said, rushing away.

Presently I heard a calm voice, strong in the noise. " I 'm short of men, doctor. Send up one of yours."

I motioned to Brown, who without a word went above. Just then I felt something trickling on my face, and looking up saw the planking above had sprung, and a red stream was breaking through.

" For heaven's sake put me out of this," came one of the voices. I was bending over him, when again Captain Perry sang out, —

" Brown is down. Send another."

It was not five minutes before the same voice came : " Another," while a spar crashed.

" Who the devil, sir, is going to look after these chaps ? " I sang out.

" How many are you ? "

" Two, and some fifty men to look after."

" Can any of the wounded ? "

" They are a bad lot, sir."

" Come yourself, Mr. Moran."

I turned from my patient. I indeed could do little there. The cries and groans of these poor chaps sickened me. One of them, the Narragansett Indian, Pohig, suddenly rose, when he was pinned a writhing mass against the side.

" Go, Mr. Moran," Usher said in a husky whisper; and I turned and fled, and slipped in the gloom above, — for the thick smoke had left the deck not less dim than the mess-room. Bodies were piled everywhere; gun carriages on their sides as if carelessly tossed; and whizzing and bursting sounds about my ears.

Mr. Taylor came slipping and limping across the deck.

" Here, — at that gun ! "

" Here ! " said the captain himself.

" He was erect in the boat, still regardless of the
whizzing balls."

The Colors of the " Lawrence "

There were three of us training that gun : Mr. Pierce, the chaplain, the purser, and I, the surgeon ; and close beside it, his face staring into the smoke, lay my assistant, Brown.

I think I swore, but the chaplain at this unclerical work did not reprove me. I remember I said : " Curse a ship that has to use a mess-room above the water-line for a cock-pit." I was thinking of the twenty-four-pounders which had carried poor Lamb and the Indian Pohig into eternity. And then, as we were training the gun, a voice was in our ears :

" You need n't. It 's our last gun."

Mr. Field, the purser, rose from his knees. The chaplain, I saw, had a tear on his face ; but then he was a minister. As for me, I looked up at the blue flag.

Captain Perry seemed to read me.

" Yes, the ship, but not the battle. Yarnell, lower a boat."

" You will leave us ? " said I.

" For the ' Niagara,' " and he pointed

to her looming near through the fog. I understood.

" But the ' Lawrence ? ' " said I.

The boat had been lowered. I remember I heard a voice, —

" But the flag, captain ? "

He too looked up there where his flag still waved. The man who hauled that down, threw the blue flag after it.

Then I heard something like a sob. Now, I don't mind a man yelling with pain, for it is my trade to hear that ; but a man sobbing cuts into my heart ; and this cry came from Mr. Yarnell, one of the bravest officers that ever served. He looked queer enough, as we all did, — not more than twenty left, all told ; our faces black as the negroes', and tracked with perspiration ; our bodies smeared with soot and blood ; our clothes torn.

But Captain Perry put his hand on his shoulder.

" We must have the day, Yarnell. What is the ' Lawrence ' to that ? "

Then Yarnell straightened up, and smiled through his tears and the blood trickling from a scalp wound.

" I 'll stand by the ' Lawrence,' captain."

The captain gave us all a cheering look as he leaped over the side. I wondered whether this was the same man who three hours before (I have learned since that it was just two hours and forty-five minutes) had talked to me in the cabin. And I remembered the packet he had given me, which I had stuffed away in a drawer in that terrible cock-pit, —

" Shall I sink the papers ? "

" Yes, if it comes to that," he sang back ; and the last I saw he was erect in the boat, still regardless of the whizzing balls, and his brother at his side, and the four men bending to their oars. His figure gave me new spirit, and I remembered Usher at his hard duty in the cock-pit. As I stumbled to the passage, Yarnell stopped me.

The Colors of the " Lawrence "

" We can't stand this."

I looked up at the Stars and Stripes, still flying, if the other flags were lacking.

" We have lost half our colors, and we must the rest ? " said I, like a man in a bad dream. The colors seemed that moment more to me than all those dead and wounded and the wrecked ship.

" They 're battering us to pieces. Must n't we save these few ? "

And he pointed to those left standing.

" We must make the wounded comfortable, too."

" But the colors," gasped another voice, when turning I saw Midshipman Dulany Forest ; and then I remembered, and answered fiercely, —

" It 's not the colors now. We 're beaten, man."

But I could not endure seeing it done, loudly as I had spoken ; and without lifting my eyes I went to my work ; and such work as it was I do not care even to think about now. Then directly the crashing above paused. The colors were down, that meant; and I heard a low cheer over the water from the king's ship; but with us only were the groaning men, and Mr. Forest's spaniel howled, as he had since the crash in the china closet.

As for me I did not dare think, I say. I had enough to do, Heaven knows. The sight of poor shattered Mr. Brooks, who had been always my good friend, took away the little spirit I had left. But finally I was so faint that again I stumbled on deck; and there I saw Mr. Yarnell directing the raising of our colors. Yes, that flag was going up over the " Lawrence " again.

" What does it mean ? " I asked; but I saw in a glance.

" That the ' Niagara ' has borne down through their line, and the fight has turned."

" He reached the ' Niagara ' then ? "

You know how it was. The " Queen Charlotte," in trying to bring her broad-

side in play on the " Niagara," had been
left at the wind's mercy through a down-
haul having been shot away, and so she
had fouled the " Detroit." The " Niagara," backing her main topsails, had run
across bow and stern of the two fouled
king's ships, tearing them fore and aft
with her starboard broadside ; and keeping
on, she paid the " Lady Prevost " the same
attention. Our " Caledonia," " Ariel,"
" Somers," " Scorpion," " Tigress," and
" Porcupine " had followed, carrying away
the " Detroit's " masts and the " Queen
Charlotte's " mizzenmast. And as I came
on deck, the " Niagara " was engaging the
" Hunter."

" You see I think I am right about running up the colors," said Yarnell.

" That looks as if you were," said I,
pointing to the " Hunter's " taffrail, where
an officer was waving a white handkerchief
from a boarding spike. Again he waved
it ; and we knew we had won the Lakes.

But the groans on our deck took away

our cheers, and I turned to that work.
Now, you must know I had not been long
away; for all this decisive part of the
action was a matter of but eight minutes.
They were precious moments, I can assure
you, with all the arms and legs and heads
I had to bandage.

"He's coming back," said Mr. Pierce,
the chaplain, coming to us at this dismal
task, for I had lost all of my professional zest.

"Who?" said I, dully.

"The captain, and the flags."

"Let me see him, the captain!" said
the man I was tending, — "back again, is
he?"

"You can't," said I. "Keep still."

"But I will."

And he tottered up despite us, reminding me of Perkins, the petty officer, who
had done the same earlier in the action,
whose body lay by a starboard gun.

"Usher," said I, "I must see his flag
go up!" I spoke like a child.

" But these ? " he said reproachfully.

" I 'll be back. They must give us help. We can't do all this alone ; " and I put my hands to my ears to keep out their groans.

" The captain is back ? " came a voice shrilly.

" Yes, back. We 've got 'em," piped another.

" Well, I don't care so much," said a chap who had both arms shot away.

" I must take his hand," said I to my assistant, Usher, again ; " I 'll be away — well, five minutes."

" Go, of course," said the armless man. " Cheer the captain for me."

" Are ye tellin' me, we 've beat 'em, Mr. Moran ? " asked another, forgetful of pain.

" Yes, and the captain is back on the 'Lawrence,' " said I, hastening to the deck; for I declare I wanted to see that blue flag make our colors complete more than I wished a sight of that girl in New York.

The Colors of the " Lawrence "

And what a crowd were we, as we stood banded and splinted at the side; while the decks were red and slippery, and the groans of the suffering took the place of cheers. For we greeted him silently, and he himself but said, as he looked over human fragments, cannon dismounted, carriages broken, and shattered timbers:

"Put up the blue flag on the 'Lawrence,' for she was given up but to win the fight."

Battered Yarnell took his captain's hand, as he came over the side, and we crowded about him; and our hearts, if not our mouths, cheered; for his unconquerable will had gained that day what General Hull had lost. Yes, he alone had, — this boyish Master Commandant Oliver Hazard Perry. And if we did not cheer with our mouths, it was because of the groans of the suffering.

Shortly the surviving officers of the king's fleet were over the side, and looked wonderingly at the havoc they had made, and slipped in the blood, and stumbled over the bodies, as they went to deliver their swords to our captain, who returned them with civility, remembering how nearly he had lost. And above waved the two flags, — the blue with Captain Lawrence's words, which Captain Perry had made of even greater meaning.

Now I must tell you how strangely, some few minutes after this, I remembered I had forgot his order to drop the packet of official papers overboard. I left my work, and hurried to him. I believe now I was in a daze, as well I might be. He was handing a letter to Midshipman Forest.

" I forgot to sink that packet when we struck our colors," I cried.

" You did, eh ? " said he. " But the colors are up; so I'll pardon you, Mr. Moran. You see, I have just sent General Harrison these words : ' We have met the enemy, and they are ours, — two ships, two brigs, one schooner, and two sloops.' "

I turned, without a word, to my work

among the human wreckage this great lake
fight had made; and you may believe I
was kept busied for days; and Mr. Pierce,
the chaplain, too, when the leaded shrouds
were sent whirring down into the depths
of that lake for whose control these men
had given their lives.

And such is war. If the " Lawrence "
flew her colors at the end, what mattered
it to those chaps in the leaded shrouds?

The Impulsiveness of Monsieur de la Fayette

The Impulsiveness of Monsieur de la Fayette

An Account of the Affair at Barren Hill, from the Middleton Memoirs

I

MONSIEUR DE LA FAYETTE had time to look for lodgings which appeared most desirable either in the stone church, or in the house of the Quaker Peters. Peters had observed the tall, red-haired boy, who was the French marquis, with some attention. He acknowledged that his hospitality was not given willingly, for he was strictly " king's man," with small enough sympathy for the rebels or for " French gentlemen " who chose to bother with other people's affairs.

In fact, foreigners were not altogether popular, even with us. I remember how Generals Greene and Sullivan both had threatened to resign because of Congress's employment of foreign adventurers, and Washington himself had been criticised for his affection for the French stripling. Had not the " little " tall fellow made a failure of the Canadian expedition ? Yet he was a general now, admitted to all of the chief's councils, intrusted with the perilous commissions to watch the British and to stop the ravages along the Delaware. " You do not know the stuff in that French boy," the general had said to the critics. " Remember Gloucester and Brandywine ; remember that Monsieur de Vergennes's attitude has been, in some measure, brought about because a great French nobleman is interested with us."

Monsieur de Vergennes's, that is to say, Louis XVI.'s attitude, was known among us May 2, 1779. Possibly the Quaker Peters hated the youthful French gentleman the more on that account. Good English loyalists had small sympathy

Monsieur de la Fayette

for things French, and now, to add to all the ancient reasons for hatred — descending from the time when France was practically Harry of England's fief — was this acknowledgment of the colonies' rebellion. Oh, this French impertinence!

Mr. Peters fidgeted in his doorway, watching the arrangement of the twenty-one hundred men this boyish French person commanded.

The marquis, in fact, had made the Peters farm on the hill-top his position, exactly eleven miles from the enemy's at Philadelphia, and nearly the same distance from ours at Valley Forge. On his right was the Schuylkill; a rocky ledge, with three pieces of cannon, before; a wood and some stone walls and houses, making admirable breastworks, at the left, where he had put the two remaining cannon. Three hundred yards down the slope, to the front, was Captain McLane, with fifty Indians and six hundred pickets.

The marquis regarded these things complacently with General Poor, shading his eyes with his hands and looking out over the green distances to Philadelphia. Boy as he was — scarcely twenty — he felt some pride in his sense in taking the position. Of course, General Poor had agreed with him in all the details, but he had advanced the ideas. They were excellently good ones, too, he thought. The "Swedes' Ford" was down that wooded road, while behind was another not-much-used means of retreat.

"Well taken, general, I declare!" General Poor had said, and the two had separated, La Fayette walking toward Peters, who still stood regarding the scene with curious interest. The dwelling was close by the little stone church.

"I am sorry, sir, believe me, to have to intrude at your table," said Monsieur de la Fayette, coming up. As a matter of pride, he wished to speak good English, and by this time he could use the tongue well; but a slight accent lingered.

Monsieur de la Fayette

"I might say that I am only too glad to entertain the Marquis de la Fayette," Peters said; "but frankly, as a British subject, I should not be speaking the strict truth."

"Ah, I like your directness," said monsieur, gayly. "We all have a right to our opinions."

"Yes, I agree with thee, general, most completely, and, finding thee most fairminded, I am emboldened to ask of thee a favor."

"A favor, Mr. Peters?" asked monsieur, smiling, and looking the man over narrowly. He was a little man, with dark, earnest eyes, a thin, wrinkled face, to which his garb lent a certain air of peacefulness, such as monks and Quakers sometimes gain, and a suggestiveness of cleanly living and thinking. "I will grant it readily if I can."

"My daughter wishes to go through the lines," the man said, rubbing his hands together and looking away.

"The very pretty girl I saw?" asked the marquis. He had not forgotten to observe a neat face and figure.

"A good girl, sir," Peters said. "I am alone here, and do not care to have her exposed to the danger."

"But the danger of the ride?" asked Monsieur de la Fayette.

"I shall send my black servant with her."

"And why, sir, should I permit her to go into Philadelphia? Are you not a loyalist? You acknowledge it. Your daughter will explain the matter to Sir Henry, I fear."

"Fear not, friend — not at all. She will not."

And at the moment La Fayette thought he heard the shutter of the window before which they stood rattle. He remarked it to his unwilling host rather suspiciously, and then he looked the man over again. It was so easy to grant the favor. The face was honest enough. Ah, Monsieur

Monsieur de la Fayette

de la Fayette was yet young in experience!
In a long, eventful life he was to know
better. Here, in America, he was now
only beginning his experience. But I like
to think of him as he stood there at the
door of the house on the hill. I like to
think of him as impulsively generous, as
he had been in all this affair. It pleased
the Emperor Napoleon at a later date to
call him a " ninny." By a " ninny " the
emperor may have meant a man clever
only in simple honesty. I never myself
held Monsieur de la Fayette among the
most clever men, but he always was one
you could depend on exactly. Because he
never was false he suffered a deal. And
so, to return to Peters's request for permission to send his daughter into Philadelphia, he foolishly granted it. Some men
are lovable because they are foolish, and
God, after all, esteems it a finer quality
than cunning, although it may act against
worldly success.

After receiving the man's thanks Mon-

6   81

sieur de la Fayette paused to look with satisfaction at his position, all its advantages displayed by the country that lay stretched out in the late afternoon light as if 't were a map.

"And how, friend, didst thou first think of coming among us?" asked Peters.

The young man turned to him smilingly.

"Ah, I remember, now that you ask, a dinner in Metz, when His Highness the Duke of Gloucester was the guest of my commandant, the Comte de Broglie; your English prince told a story of the events here that fired my imagination."

"And yet thou hadst much property — and a wife? — how imprudent!"

"Ah, Anastasia!" said monsieur, his face growing earnest. "But, Mr. Peters, you know there is more in this world than one's money, or pleasure, or —"

"Yes, thou art right, friend — duty."

"Yes, duty. But that depends, I suppose, on how one interprets it."

"Exactly," said Peters. "Exactly."

Monsieur de la Fayette

" I suppose my friend, Sir Henry Clinton there, is quite as near right as I, although we fight on different sides of the question." And he waved his hand toward the horizon where Philadelphia lay. " I once met him in London at a ball. But if your daughter, Mistress Prudence, goes to-night, I must go in to write the pass. It's a dangerous ride in these unsettled times. Have you considered ? "

" I prefer to have her there, friend," Peters answered, averting his face, while Monsieur de la Fayette entered the house to the room that had been assigned him.

No sooner had the door closed than the shutter which he had observed move during his conversation with Peters swung open, and a blue-eyed, blond-haired face showed in the opening.

" Father, I have heard every word."

" Get thee ready, Prudence, now, in a hurry."

" And am I — "

" Thou art to go at once to Sir William

83

Howe and tell him how our French gentleman is encamped."

" I cannot."

" Cannot ? "

" He trusts us." Tears were in the
blue eyes, the lips trembled.

" Thou must go, because thou art safer
there. Thou must get word to Sir William, because our first duty is to the king.
Thou must."

Still Prudence hesitated ; still the man
reasoned, acknowledging that he indeed
had taken advantage of Monsieur de la
Fayette's youthful impulsiveness, and jus-
tifying himself because in war it is even
godly to use unfair means. How does the
pretence of godliness cloak many a selfish purpose ! Ah, but is it not ever a
perplexing matter to arrive at the exact
right ?

The man had been accustomed always
to control the girl. His was the stronger
will.

Monsieur de la Fayette standing at the

door on the hill saw the pretty Quaker maiden riding down the slope with his permit. He wondered if he had been imprudent. He took it, indeed, in good part when General Poor rated him soundly for the imprudence of that pass.

And then slowly the May night settled over lowland and hill.

In Philadelphia the Mischianza was being celebrated in honor of Sir William Howe, who just had been superseded by Sir Henry Clinton.

" Mischianza " was a clever term arrived at by that witty young gentleman, Captain André, who could write a sonnet, a play, lead a minuet, and not hesitate at daring service.

II

Among the handsomest young women of this period in Philadelphia was Miss Dorothy Mortimer. I believe Mr. Stuart's picture of her is excellent. It shows a tall, dark-haired, dark-eyed young woman, with an animated expression and a complexion of clear pallor, and exquisitely gowned in the mode the least provincial of Philadelphia during the Revolutionary period. The Mortimers were strong loyalists, and were among those Maryland families who left the United States when the affair at Yorktown had confiscated the estates of many of the losing opinion. Miss Mortimer's inclinations were supposed to be loyal. Yet, in that period when families were divided, it would not have been surprising if she had discovered sympathies for some of the other political complexion. She, indeed, appeared to have many sympathies, as a young dandy, who took her too much from her actions, found out to his cost.

When the " Mischianza " was ending in the great ball at the Wharton's, she shared much of the ardent attention of those fine young officers of Howe's, who were not long from London seasons. In the mock tournament Lord Cathcart's first aide had worn her colors, and it was this young gentleman who let drop the information, as they stood in one corner, that a pretty Quakeress below had just brought Sir William news that the little French gentleman was encamped on Barren Hill, not eleven miles away.

"Sir William will have the marquis for dinner day after to-morrow," Lieutenant Fielding repeated.

"And this girl brought the news?" Miss Mortimer asked curiously.

"She rode over from her father's farm with a black servant, I 'm told. She was brought here not a half-hour ago by her uncle, who thought she could the better describe the marquis's position."

"I wish — I wish I could see her — just to see what a girl who would dare to do such a thing can be like," said Miss Mortimer.

The minuet went on in the next room. Everybody was joyous with the wine of

the dinner and the spirit of festivity.
What could have been finer than that
occasion ? — the festival of the day and
earlier evening, the great dining-hall re-
splendent with plate and Oriental fantasies,
where the arrangement of mirrors made
the scene more dazzling by the beauty of
the women, the splendor of the men!
And now the dancing was at its height.

"Yes," said Miss Mortimer again, "I
would just like to see a girl who would do
that."

Of course she could see her, Lieutenant Fielding declared. He thought, indeed, he would have given his right arm
for her smile of approval.

"Oh, if you could!"

He could, and did. Sir William himself was not averse to doing so simple a
favor for a charming young lady. This
was his high compliment, this "Mischianza;" he only could be gracious to
everybody — and when the body chanced
to be the beautiful Miss Mortimer?

Monsieur de la Fayette

" Gad, I 'm delighted at the chance ! "

The Quakeress, her servant, and her uncle were in the room below. " A pretty, tired-faced little blond thing," Miss Mortimer decided. Sir William and Lieutenant Fielding stood in the doorway.

" I was so curious," said the beautiful Miss Mortimer, " to see you who dared to bring the news."

" I have told Sir William as well as I could," said Prudence, wondering at this beautiful lady, who seemed after the ride over the rough roads a vision out of Paradise. Miss Mortimer smiled graciously, glancing then at Sir William.

" I would wish you might leave Miss Peters with me just a moment. I want to talk with her privately."

" Certainly," said Sir William, rather wondering at what Miss Mortimer wished; still, he was in the spirit of accommodating geniality. The relative asked if Miss Mortimer wanted him and the servant to leave, too. " Why, if you don't mind,"

Miss Mortimer said. The little Quakeress looked her perplexity.

When the door was shut and they were
alone, save for the crashing music of the
military bands, Miss Mortimer's smile
passed.

" How could you ? " she asked.

Prudence began to weep.

" My father made me."

" Little fool, had you no spirit of your
own ? "

" I am afraid of him."

" Yes, I see."

Prudence fidgeted. The cool, surprising contempt in the other's words and eyes
seemed but to show her own self-deprecia-
tion, her detestation of the deed. She
could not restrain the sobs. Miss Mortimer went to the door.

" Sir William," she said, throwing it open,
" we have ended our little conversation."

Sir William entered, wonderingly. The
little Quakeress was sobbing as if her
heart would break.

Monsieur de la Fayette

" Oh ? " he began.

" She is tired out, poor child," said Miss Mortimer, calmly.

" Ah, Mr. Fielding, I'm ready to go back to the dance."

" Too bad the little girl is crying," said Fielding, when they were outside.

" Too bad," he added, " after all she has done. Through that news Sir William expects to catch the little marquis like a rat in a trap."

" Yes, exactly like a rat in a trap," said Miss Mortimer, laughing. " But don't you think women queer ? "

" Ah, yes, Miss Mortimer! I never thought about it. Who were you thinking of ? "

" Oh, of myself."

" Oh, I say, if to be adorable is to be queer —" he began.

But at the moment Lord Cathcart claimed her.

Two hours later she sat, in her ball-gown still, writing at a little desk. The

dawn lit the room so that she could follow
the pen.

DEAR JIM [it ran], — A weak little Quaker
thing has just ridden in and told the whole secret
of the position.   Sir Henry Erskine and General
Grant are already on the road to cut off your
rear and to occupy the " Swedes' Ford."   Sir
Henry himself goes with four thousand more by
the Germantown road.   Sir William has boasted
he will have the marquis to dinner to-morrow
night, and that he will ship with him to London.
Look out !   DOROTHY.

This was all.   She arose and looked out
of the window over the lawn.   The May
dawn left her older, faded — the beautiful
Miss Mortimer !

" Is it worse for her — or me ? "

She paused, her hands crossed behind
her.

" But —"

Would they be caught by Sir William
like rats in a trap ?

Monsieur de la Fayette

III

Monsieur de la Fayette had been busy all that day strengthening his position and rearranging his lines and his scouts. Up at dawn as he had been, he now felt fagged, and so had thrown himself down on his bed at Quaker Peters's, when suddenly his door was thrown open without warning by Captain Jim Trelawney, of Poor's.

"General!" cried Trelawney, breathing hard.

"*Le diable!*" said the general, raising his head from the bed and rubbing his eyes.

"Your pass to the Quakeress has betrayed us!"

"Betrayed us!" cried the marquis in his turn, now on his feet.

For answer Trelawney led him to the window.

"Do you see the scarlet moving yonder?"

"The dragoons we expect," said La Fayette, peering out.

"So I thought until I had a letter."

"A letter?"

"A letter brought by a family servant of my cousin in Philadelphia telling us that the Quakeress you passed has betrayed us."

"Impossible!" cried the marquis, and then he paused: "I've had, I think, Captain Trelawney, a lesson in human nature."

At the moment there was a step in the hall. Monsieur de la Fayette rushed out, dragging in his host.

"Villain! you sent word by your daughter to the British!"

"I did," said the man, calmly.

"You lied to me!"

"I lied."

"And why?"

"Because, friend, I am a British subject, as thou art a French one."

"*Peste!*" cried La Fayette. "You

made me play the fool! Arrest him, captain!" he ordered Trelawney, and then was outside before the church, where he met General Poor and Captain Mc-Lane running toward him. Recollecting himself, his folly, his lack of self-control, he began to smile like a courtier.

"We are surrounded!"

"I know it."

"They have occupied ' Swedes' Ford.'"

A thousand devils! had they? But again, —

"I know."

"What are we to do?"

"Wait; I will tell you."

But could he? He must. He could not endure this after the dismal Canadian failure. But he must smile. Suddenly, as will sometimes happen in moments of great perplexity, a clarity followed.

"Throw forward false heads of columns, as if we were going to give battle."

"There are nine thousand of them!"

"False heads, I ordered!—as feints. We are to withdraw."

"But the 'Swedes' Ford' is already occupied."

"I know it," said the marquis; "I know it. I propose to make only a pretence of giving battle while we withdraw the men by Matson's Ford."

Matson's Ford, indeed, remained; they recollected that, regaining their respect for their commander.

The men were withdrawn, Poor's first, while the enemy waited, deceived by the false heads of the columns. As these false heads began to withdraw, the front lines of the British pushed in on them. Just then Captain McLane's Indians sprang out from their ambush, whooping and so frightening some of the chasseurs, who thought they were devils, that they never stopped running until they reached Philadelphia. The false heads became tails. They were running before the British, who gave them a brisk volley. But the little army was now mostly across the river, drawing in line on the hill there. The British columns, coming together on the abandoned Barren Hill, met but each other.

That little French fellow had escaped.

Monsieur de la Fayette, in fact, had no longer to force a smile.

He had made a fairly good retreat. Before overwhelming numbers he had lost no more than eleven. He laughed to himself as he stood on the hill in the new position.

Calling his aide, Captain Trelawney, he asked : —

" Well ? "

" Prettily done, general ! "

" *Merci ! merci !* Yet, my dear captain, that letter of your cousin's came just in time. It was considerate of him — "

" Of her," interrupted the captain.

" A woman ! " ejaculated Monsieur de la Fayette.

" A very charming woman, general," said the captain.

" Ah, I 'm quite ready to believe that," said the marquis. " But, really, the situation is astounding. We are betrayed by one woman and saved by another !" But, as a Gaul, he soon began to hold this as but one more experience among many.

Miss Mortimer had a visitor that evening in the person of Lieutenant Fielding.

" And did they catch the marquis ? "

" No, no, I believe not. The fact is, he got away very, very cunningly. He's rather more of a chap than we thought."

" Oh, is he ? " said Miss Mortimer, smiling. " And how about some women, pray ? "

" Some are false. I have Shakespeare's authority."

" Ah, yes, some, Mr. Fielding. But could anything have been more amusing than the dance last night ? "

She looked flushed and very good-natured,

Monsieur de la Fayette

and Lieutenant Fielding wondered a bit at
the reason.   Women always furnished the
lieutenant a perplexity, in which he certainly delighted, or else he never would
have indulged in so many experiments.

The Extreme Edge of Hazard

The Extreme Edge of Hazard

A soldier's a man ;
A life's but a span —

Othello.

His end was so glorious, that I protest not even his mother or his mistress ought to have deplored it, or at any rate wished him alive again. I know it is a hero we speak of; and yet I vow I scarce know whether in the last act of his life I admire the result of genius, invention, and daring, or the boldness of a gambler winning surprising odds. — THACKERAY, in *The Virginians.*

AT QUEBEC, 17th *October*, 1759.

SO long it is, my dear Will, since we have had much time for penmanship, that now I am not quite sure how to hold a quill. This is an old sputtering point at the best; and, between that and an arm just recovering from a musket wound, I think you will have a passably hard time in deciphering what I am now putting to paper in this wretched, dismantled town. I look out over the wintry plain and the winding river bank where our batteries were. Now men and batteries and battalions have sailed, all, and we are left alone and dismal — a set of ragged heroes — in the fortress for which we fought so long and despairingly. Ah, Will, I'm sick at heart! You in Surrey may be happy, or in London at a coffee-house, or at a rout near a powdered face (I swear you are very near it, if it be pretty); but here's only the sorry desolation of war, and dismal folk, and sour-faced infantrymen, and nothing to do in particular. Some, of course, amuse themselves in the garrison with play — there are men who would gamble in heaven or — the other place; but I detest cards almost as much as poor Jim Wolfe, who swore that the one game he could abide was piquet, because his mother played it. (I believe the only time he ever played was with that good woman, whom he adored in the same degree that he disliked cards.) Dear Jim Wolfe, Will, whom we used to love and quarrel with as boys; whom we knew so well; who had so frail a body and so mighty a spirit; who could madden you with his irritability, and again charm you with the sweetness of his changing temper; who would not surrender to adverse circumstance!

At the last, when all were croaking, Admiral Saunders said that he must put down the river, for winter was coming on; and the council declared, with long-drawn, deprecatory faces, for abandoning the siege.

Then poor Jim, our great Jim, General Jim, Will, thrust his hands in his belt, and walked up and down the room, his face pale, his eyes sunk (for he was off a sickbed, and God knows how he could be there at all). "Gentlemen, we've had bad luck enough. I'll say nothing of Montmorency, and I have assured Admiral Saunders there that I was in the wrong — not he. But, God helping us, I say we must be, we will be on that height! Oh, I mean it!" said he, with a kind of quaver in his voice. "At least we'll have a last shy at the Canadas."

"And if that be only a shy?" asked one.

"Barring the few we shall leave on the Isle-aux-Coudres, all will sail down the river," said the general. He had stopped his saunter then, his fingers still in his belt, and they thought him trembling a little; till suddenly he turned about — this dear, ugly, sickly Jim, that we used to know rather differently (though always ugly) — and stalked out of the room. "How does he keep up?" murmured one. "How do we all keep up?" said Saunders, looking out of the window, where then a shell, off the Beauport shore, sailed with a long tail of light across the sky. Jack Jervis told me this afterward, whispering, "That man makes me sick!"

And we went off together to our duty, for the council was over for the day.

The Extreme Edge of Hazard

That day! How long it seems gone! Heaven knows when you may get this letter. Our mail service is not of the best. But the Canadas are England's through Mr. Pitt's strategy. Not the least of the great man's intuitions was choosing our Jim for general.

The particulars of the next days you know well, Will, by this time: how Montmorency was abandoned; how Montcalm and Monsieur Vaudreuil were put in some perplexity by our feints. We were preparing for departure, and the last attack; though I, no more than any of us, knew what that was to be. The going up and down the river with the ebb and flow, the apparent descents on Bougainville's forces, — these movements perplexed our sailors and soldiers as much as they apparently mystified those Frenchmen, with their painted savages and *voyageurs des bois*. I was working hard then. You would not have known me, Will. One had little time for sleep. As they say the Marquis

The Extreme Edge of Hazard

de Montcalm said of himself, we were always " in our boots." Again the general was everywhere, observing, taking account of all that was done. But more was to be done, and what that was we whispered and talked over, Colonel Burton and I, at Point Levi.

The twelfth, I think, Colonel Burton himself came to me, as I sat over some hard bread and a mug of the poorest beer. (Its taste was delicious, Will.) " To-morrow is the day, Sir Charles," said he, shaking his great-coat, for it was raining.

" To-morrow," said I, on my feet.

" To-night for you, my lad. A boat is waiting off shore to take you to the ' Porcupine.' "

" From the general ? "

" From the general, Sir Charles. You are relieved here. I am to march down the south shore to a point opposite Anse-de-Foulon."

" The general is with Captain Jervis, then ? "

The Extreme Edge of Hazard

"On the 'Porcupine,'" said the colonel.
"Good-night, Sir Charles."

He paused, rather brusquely, I thought.

"We have said 'good-by' several times
in the last three months."

"But there has always been a 'good-
morning' for us," said I.

"Humph, we are wicked, perhaps. Several better fellows than you or I never said
the 'good-morning,'" answered Burton,
shaking his coat again.

And I was in the "Porcupine's" boat,
the oars rising and falling in the black
water, the night now and then broken by
the artillery. Above on the heights the
quiet was singular. 'T was from below
that suddenly a flashing shell might burst
over the river.

"There 're twenty-three offered," I
heard a petty officer forward say.

"For what?" said I, turning.

"To lead in the enterprise, sir."

"The enterprise!" I muttered.

"It's them that need n't pray, and are

not afraid of hell, sir," said the man.
"Twenty-four are wanted. Hark ye,
what's that?"

But I had no need of listening. Our
ears were deafened with the steady roll of
guns far down the stream.

"On the Beauport shore," said the men.

Did you ever see the blackness of a
rainy, dismal night so lit, Will? Ah, you
never did.

"Admiral Saunders is stirring up the
Moosirs, sir," said my acquaintance in
the bow.

But, as it proved, neither Captain Jervis
nor the general was on the "Porcupine,"
where word had been left for us to proceed
to Admiral Holmes's ship. It took a good
bit of rowing before we came within reach
of the "Sutherland," and the air was filled
with moist, gunpowdery smells, and deafening reports, not alone from below but
from above toward Monsieur Bougainville's position. The Frenchies were kept
awake that night, except one Vergor at

The Extreme Edge of Hazard

Anse-de-Foulon, who was a poltroon; —
but of him later.

A little midshipman saluted, and told
me the general waited me below. As I
stepped into the cabin the sudden glare of
candles blinded me. Then I saw Jim, our
old Jim, and Jack Jervis. They were
alone, and very quiet. Jim's face was sunk
in his hands. When he looked up I saw
his eyes were strangely bright, like those
of one with fever, while his cheeks kept
their pallor.

"You 're wet, Charlie," Jack Jervis said.

"Rain 's as comfortable as powder,"
said I, throwing aside my top-coat.

"Do you wish you were in England,
Charlie? I almost wish it myself!" said
our friend the general.

"'T is a pleasant thought," said I, softly;
"yes, pleasant."

"Back in the old place — think of it!"
The noise outside kept up apace. "Out
of the infernal hubbub," he said wearily.
But his tone changed.

The Extreme Edge of Hazard

"Jervis and you, Charlie, are good chaps — good friends when you are friends. I swear you will have another career some day than the army. I believe you're here now because old John Beechwood thought I'd look after you a bit."

"Out of the spirit of adventure, Jim," said I.

"But what has it led to? Only to disgrace, defeat. Your uncle chose a sorry fellow to be guardian."

"Your pains have reached to your brain, Jim," Jervis said, with a hand on his shoulder.

"Likely! Likely! I swear at my body sometimes. I'd better swear at my follies ; though I believe those bitter days at Iverness counted for as much against me. I was a fool — often."

But when we tried to interrupt him, he laughed, his humor changing, as it did so wondrous fast at times, so that it took ready wit to follow him.

"Oh, don't bother. I have a plan.

The Extreme Edge of Hazard

There's a slanting path up Anse-de-Foulon."

" And twenty-four go forward. Let me be leader," I cried, catching at his spirit.

" But you must not. I intended ordering you down to Admiral Saunders, Charlie."

" Go I must, Jim ! You must let me," I cried. " Let me have my share of the glory — "

" Or the ignominy — "

" Or the disgrace, with you, Jim."

" But how can I ? Did not your uncle, that gruff old John Beechwood, do me many a favor ? Shall I put his nephew in the way of dying — or of a heroism, maybe ? "

" For that reason let me go with you," I said again. " Oh, Jim, don't deny me. Let me have command of the twenty-four. And let my men follow. I may not be so good an officer. I may be younger than Murray, or Townsend, or Monckton ! But — "

The Extreme Edge of Hazard

"You shall have it, Charlie. Yes, man, you shall have it. I'll order yours from the south shore with Burton. If I succeed you'll thank me. If I fail again you can no more than share the dishonor."

"I wish I were in it," said Jervis. "I wish ——"

"You must do something else for me, Jack," our Jim said. Then I saw he had something in his hand; and when he turned it to the light it proved to be a little portrait — painted very neatly, Will — of Kate Lowther. There, in the cabin of the admiral's ship, on the stormy, tumultuous night, was your cousin's miniature. And, indeed, it had been in all that long siege, because our ugly, dear general had worn it always.

"Give it her, Jack. That's all."

"But you will yourself."

"The chance is against me."

"Shall I say anything beyond?" said Jervis. He was rather clumsy that night, I think because he liked our friend, though we had been through so much, and together had laughed at death, and seen it at its worst — when some poor devil was crying in agony of a wound a thousand times keener than the direct thrust.

" Oh, she will know," said Jim. " She is one of the women who understand."

Nor did we smile at this lover-like remark, as we might have in a lighter mood, when at home, or in camp, some one passed the jesting story. So with unchallenged and unusual sentiment he continued : —

" I never believed in women till that time at Bath, and — there's no woman like her, Jack."

" I will keep it till you ask for it, Jim."

" Till I ask for it ! Why, sir, I don't believe I could drag myself back to England with this poor old body, should we get through — should we — "

He turned to us both then.

" You shall lead the twenty-four, Charlie, up the slope alone. Good-bye, Jack."

The Extreme Edge of Hazard

A knock came at the door. " Major Stobo," said the aide-de-camp.

" Wait," the general said to me. "Ask General Monckton and Admiral Holmes to come below." These entered directly, not hiding entirely their distrust of the leader's despairing plan. He told them I had asked to lead the volunteers, and that my men should follow with Colonel Burton, for, he was pleased to say, my past service deserved this post. Will, he had ever a prejudice in a friend's favor.

The details you may know : how we understood a provision convoy was to be sent by Bougainville, and how in the darkness we swung stilly down stream, I in the foremost boat, nervous and not quite myself, he at my side. Below, the guns of Saunders still sounded, but about was only the dip of oars.

If Bougainville's men noted, they doubtless thought it the usual feigning ; so many times had they seen our boats go up and down with ebb and flow. Our general was very still, but I heard his voice muttering something, I think, of Gray, the poet :

" The paths of glory lead but to the grave."

As boys, we should have laughed at him; but in earnest danger there 's incongruity in the farcical, though I have known the contrary.

" I wish I could have written such a line," said he.

I might have told him he could write a better; but one thought not of wit or discussion then. Our general talked his verse, as he was so earnest a soul, Will — so changeable in means, and yet so steadfast at his main end; all the apparent changes were only to the set purpose. He would not be defeated. And at last he was taking what seemed simply the fool's chance. And we were eager to follow him — even those among us (not I, Will, you know) who, because he was not of noble birth, disliked to serve him who had won his own distinction.

The Extreme Edge of Hazard

At the left, the dark cliffs enveloped the enterprise with added gloom. The tumult from the Beauport shore far below quieted, when suddenly a hoarse voice cried : —

" Qui vive ? "

" France ! " I answered, in the tongue you and I acquired at the Embassy in Paris, Will.

" A quel Régiment ? "

" De la Reine ! " I cried again.

We held our very breaths, for supposing the provision convoy, told of by the deserters, had passed ! But chance (God knows no chance, as the clergy say) favored. Bougainville, though we did not know this till the events long after, had countermanded his order, but had not sent notice 'long shore.

" They are deceived," whispered Colonel Fraser at my elbow. The general himself did not stir, for I stood close by him ; when suddenly, with terrible distinctness, another challenge rang out from the heights : —

The Extreme Edge of Hazard

" Qui vive ? "

For an instant the tongue clave to the roof of my mouth; and then, in the accent you used to compliment, Will, I said again : —

" France; de la Reine." In louder tone I cried to that challenger to hold his tongue. " Pour le Roi," the ship " Hunter " hung close mid-stream. Would they believe ? Can you imagine, Will, how the oars strained in the stillness ? But there was only the soughing water, and the pelting rain that froze on the cheeks. Around Anse-de-Foulon the boats pulled, on and on. Again we heard Saunders's batteries; and firing behind, farther up. Our boat grated on the pebbles, and the general and I leapt to the shore, tumbling and slipping over the icy stones. Above, far above the head-land, were scattered lights.

For a moment I pressed Jim's hand, while the volunteers crowded at my heels. " Up, every man as he may," I said, I think; and I was pulling myself up the slippery precipice, catching the bushes, sliding back, and crawling forward. I could have sworn I was hours in that steep way, though really I suppose the time could not have been longer than a quarter hour. At last the long climb ended, and I was breathless in a level space, surrounded by the little band, every man catching a gasping breath. Before I, indeed, could say a word, a half dozen sprang forward toward a cluster of tents, where the twinkling lights were. On the height a darkish dawn began to declare itself. Running with my men we heard cries before, saw some springing from the tents. One, in a long white night-robe, I pricked in the heel with a pistol shot,—the very Captain Vergor, as I found from his broken explanation. My men came struggling with two others, caught half-dressed and rubbing their heavy eyes. "You slept too well, captain," said I to the prisoner.

"You are ze vakeful ones," spoke this little dark trembling fellow. The rain was now in torrents; but the dawn already showed the files of red coats forming behind; and there was our Jim, Will — his feebleness all gone.

"Quick! We must stop that!" he said, pointing to a height where firing had begun. "It 's on our boats." That, my dear Will, the battery at Samos Point, a score of us silenced.

The rain was pelting, I have said; but no man minded the wetting of the dismal, hopeful morning. Not an enemy was now in sight since the battery at Samos had been choked. Company after company filed up the narrow path to the height. Three small pieces, drawn up over many obstacles, formed our artillery. The general paced up and down, erect, pale, wet, — the keen, alert leader. We, the followers, felt repaid for all those months of ineffectual effort and inaction, for now we should achieve something. Yet we were in a most critical position. Bougainville was behind; Quebec before. Everywhere, not-

ing every company, exchanging a word
with some little officer, was the general.

Yet mostly he was silent, looking over
his ground; and at last we knew that
among the bushes and the cornhills of the
plain between the St. Charles and the
St. Lawrence our line was to be made.
Though Colonel Burton and the rest of
Webb's formed the reserve, the general
placed me with Monckton and Murray in
the van. The place we had so struggled
for was not a mile away; but a little ridge
(these Canadians called it the *Buttes à
Neveu*) intervened. I was arranging my
men when a white plume appeared above
this line; a startled cry, a "Vive le roi!"
We blazed away, and saw their heels over
the slope, while the Highland slogan followed as glibly as their own facile tongues
and as easily as their nimble legs.

So Monsieur Guienne's frightened de-
tachment carried the news, I suppose, to
Monsieur Ramsey in the town, and to
Monsieur Vaudreuil and the marquis. We

had some little firing in the rear from Bougainville, and it fell still again. In all, some forty-eight hundred stood on that highland against all the Canadas. If they had known, how easily they might have cut us off. But they did not suspect. They could not understand that the general so dared fate. And his cool presumption won. It's difficult sometimes to separate foolhardiness from designing bravery.

I think, dear Will, his ardor animated every man of us. Once I had word of him in the wait, while we stood challenged.

"I am sorry you're here, Charlie," said he in the tones of our old days; "for it's death."

"Or glory," said I, almost repeating our words in the cabin of the "Sutherland."

"Glory's a phrase," said Jim. "It brings it to us to do as well as you."

"But they all have done well," said I. "Even you, Jim!"

The Extreme Edge of Hazard

"Humph!" said he, smiling — when some duty interrupted.

And how could they help it in such a crisis, when their nerves were stretched to highest tension? Men are not cowards when nerves tingle.

But all this you know, Will; how every man of us, down to a gunner, waited a hard fight, and death perhaps. Now the great marquis — for great he was, Will, though a Frenchman — decided to charge alone. It seemed as if God in heaven watched us that day, and granted our leader the guerdon of his daring.

From the bushes, from the ground, were puffs of smoke, savages, and *voyageurs des bois*, and white uniformed skirmishers. The little cannon answered; but we stood still, firm and composed, waiting, waiting.

I saw far off a man on a dark bay horse, brandishing a sword, his wide sleeves flapping in the wind. The clouds parted, the strong light falling on him;

and 't was dark again, with the rain in our faces. "Montcalm," whispered one.

Our skirmishers were thrown before, behind; the light infantry called forward. Still we stood immovable in the van. We heard cries and musketry to the right and left. To the ground we fell (it's long after Braddock's, Will). Our hard-earned field-pieces did their work. A captain — one Tom Terwilliger, whom you knew, Will — rolled over on my right. And over the ridge we saw the enemy coming, the Canadians on the left, the regulars in the middle. On they strode, shouting, gesticulating, as the French way is. Captain Terwilliger groaned. I was too excited to notice him till, suddenly, I saw the general kneeling by his side, and feeling his pulse as if he were some dear friend, and saying gently : —

"I'm sorry, captain, sorry — we'll have you easier directly. Bravely, captain, you have won promotion." He

turned to me, " Tell Monckton to remember that, should I fail."

" Thank ye, sir," gasped poor Terwilliger. " I 'm sorry that devilish bullet
knocked me."

They appeared to stumble over each
other, and from my distance I believe I
could distinguish how each called on and
swore by his particular saint. A Canadian and a white coat would rise out of
the *mêlée*, the Canadian firing, falling to
the ground to reload; those behind tumbling over him with more invocations to the
saints to curse obstructions, and us in particular.

" Forward ! " was the word to us.

" Halt ! "

Perfectly still we stood, the disordered
French line almost upon us. They were
at our musket-tips when the order came.
For an instant I was deaf, Will; the roar
was like the explosion from a magazine;
and when the smoke cleared — God save
me from ever seeing a sight more horrid !

The Extreme Edge of Hazard

Body was piled on body. Men cursed and struggled. In a manlier tone we returned their cries, the Highlander outyelling us all: " England ! " " God save the king ! " On we bore, on and on, the line behind pushing us as if we had wished to lag. Excitement carried us in a kind of frenzy. Men fought hand-to-hand, and fell — to rise again, and fight.

In some way I found myself in a clear space — I know not how I came there. I tried to raise my right arm once, but for the first time in this life it refused the order. My writing will show that musket ball, I think, Will, if nothing else. But then I did n't feel it or care at all. I still ran till I found myself almost alone, away from the crowd, and stumbling across one sitting on the ground. " The general ! " called Lieutenant Brown of the Grenadiers. " Look out, man, the general has fallen, and ye 'll run him down." " Jim," I said then, coming to my senses. Four others were about him. I blessed the chance bringing me there.

"Lift him up, you fools!" I cried. For the first time the arm gave a horrible twitch, as I kneeled toward him, who appeared so spent.

"It's all over with me. Look to the enemy!"

"They are looked to, sir," said Brown, who, glancing up, shaded his eyes with his hand; and, forgetting all, broke into a cry:

"God, how they run!"

As gently as we could we lifted the leader in our arms; but this hurt him, and almost reverently we placed him on the ground again. Then as men may with ebbing vitality, he raised his head convulsively — his eyes quite keen and sparkling.

"Who run?"

"The enemy, sir."

"Quick!" cried Jim, "tell Colonel Burton to march Webb's down to the Charles Bridge."

"Go!" I whispered to the lieutenant of

the Grenadiers. I would not leave him then. Jim's eyes seem to comprehend me.

"And you, my Charlie? Are ye quite alive?"

"As alive as you, Jim. Ah, you must not be hurt!"

"But hurt I am. You'll see Kate Lowther?"

"Yes, Jim."

"Oh, it was Jervis who was to do that favor instead. You're here, Charlie; you would be here — and they run!"

"They run."

"God be praised — It's over!"

For a moment he lay quite still, and not many moments after, "it was well with him," as some Latin or Greek poet — I swear I can't remember which — we read it when we were boys — said of the dead.

Of course you expected so much of him, and knew him better, as the dearest fellow. If faults he had many, we understood these to like them, because they were Jim's.

The Extreme Edge of Hazard

You, as well as I, knew the dull, unconquerable perseverance which would not
yield, however the world went. On a
little thread of chance he hung his last
hope, and won glory for England, and
for himself — some talk at home, and
a monument.

The rest you know. The marquis, too,
was dead. We marched at last into his
poor broken strong place, and here Murray decided that I should remain. And
here I am, rather sad, with a bad right
arm, and shattered health, and a serious
attack of *ennui*. When I think of England so far away, sometimes I'm heart-
sick. I think of you in the minuet, and
I see all of your life. I swear I can hear
Molly's voice, and feel Ajax's cold nose
against my fingers — and see his dumb,
dog's eyes. (Perhaps he is dead by this
time.) But I think you have had enough
of this, when you may get it in the dear
old house. You will have no need to
think of poor glorious Jim. The world

thinks of him now. Ah, if he only knew! I think he might be repaid for all his disappointments. But he dared, he won; and is no longer conscious of what he won.

It's snowing outside. An icy wind blows up from the river. We find it lonely enough, and cold enough. But I suppose we should not care for these things — we have won the Canadas! Yet I don't believe we think so much of having done that as you. We wish we had some better beef and sweeter beer, and that we could see some people across the seas.

My remembrance to your cousins, the Lowthers; and with love to you and y'rs, I am

Y'rs affec'ly and ob'ntly,

CHARLES.

The Decoy Despatch

The Decoy Despatch

I CAN remember it so well that the whole scene is before me as vividly as if it were now, and I can go over my own questionings as the matter was put. It was, indeed, the Jersey Prison-ship, the Sugar House, or this. It was to be tied, when I, who always had been, again might be free. And, more, I should gain some comfort of riches, when I and mine always had slaved to poverty. Around me in the place I had left was filth, scurvy; and now, as Ratham put it, I could be done with this and be free to go as I wished.

"Why, man, it's as easy for you as walking. Do you suppose I should hesitate? Not I."

And he gave me from under his beetling brows a smile of good-will that I knew was but cunning show; for it was only his eyes that smiled, his face fixed.

" It may be easy for you," said I, bitterly. " You are of the other side."

" Yes, frankly," said he, " I am for the king, and I should not be asking you this if I were not. Yet — "

" Yet ? " said I, grasping at any excuse.

" I am a man of property; you, abominably poor. If I were in your place I would think twice, for it means an hundred pounds. An hundred pounds is not to be had easily — in peace or war."

" No," said I, reflecting. With that hundred pounds I might ask Peggy. What, after all, was all this question to me personally ? I was sergeant, but the pay was poor; had no particular prospect, whichever side won, for I ever had small wit at trading or saving. And I might — with that hundred pounds — I might start a " public " somewhere, and I might have the reason for asking Peggy; and then, besides, it meant freedom. I, who liked the woods and fields, could not bear being cooped. Why should n't I take the chance?

"Why should n't you?" asked Ratham, reading my thought.

Ah, why should n't I? If I were rich or influential I should be exchanged, but as it was I might rot. But could I do this thing? My friends were with Congress.

"Equally your friends are loyalists," Ratham said, again reading me, although I had said nothing.

Yes, that might be. Half of New York was Tory, and I had been brought up on Ratham's land. I knew him, but not as well as he me, — his cleverness; how hard he ever had been with his tenants; how strong he was; how determined for the king.

"Well, shall I take you to Sir William?"

The chance beckoned.

"Yes," said I, sullenly; and then gladly, "I'll take it."

The Decoy Despatch

" But what," said he, eying me curiously, " if you betray us ? "

" I have given my word," said I — " to the devil."

" Oh, I beg your pardon, Philip," said he. " I know you." Yes, he knew me, heart and soul, as he knew all men. " Come ; we 'll to Sir William."

And I followed him out on to Broadway, where the sun was bright and the street gay with the crowd. Only the blackened ruins of Trinity showed what war had done. These gay London and New York gentlemen, these Tory ladies, were as contemptuous of the war with their festivities as if the land were not suffering.

And I breathed the air, glad of my decision. I should have money, be free. And the service was easy — but to carry a decoy despatch ! And what, indeed, did it matter ? Must not every man aid himself? Is not the first rule self-preservation ? It 's a sorry struggle with the world at the best; a sorry fight to keep one's probity. Everything is fair when the world is against one.

We found Sir William writing. I felt awe of the great man, who looked me over as he might, in a good humor, a soldier in the ranks.

" This is our friend ? " he asked. " He is trustworthy ? "

At this I liked not my mission so well; to be trustworthy to them meant being untrustworthy to the others. Therein is the whole complex definition of untrustworthiness.

" Listen," said the general, as if he were convinced: " this letter is addressed to General Burgoyne. It reads: ' If, according to my expectations, we may succeed in getting possession of Boston, I shall without loss of time proceed to co-operate with you in the defeat of the rebel army opposed to you. Clinton is sufficiently strong to amuse Washington and Putnam. I am now making demonstrations to the southward, which, I think, will make the full effect in carrying our plan into execution.' I read it, because you would better know its purport, which is to deceive the rebels as to our plans. It's to fall into General Putnam's hands — do you understand?"

"He does, your excellency," Ratham said for me, when I answered, like a poll-parrot, "I understand." Sir William watched me a moment, and then, with a gesture, dismissed us.

"Here's the money," said Ratham outside, counting a hundred sovereigns bearing King George's likeness. "You never will earn money so easily." I looked at the gold and at him, whom I loathed.

Yet with the glitter of those pieces my last compunction vanished. What is there about gold that the yellow of it burns into the brain? I suddenly held Ratham not in such poor esteem.

And then I was started, thinking of these things.

The Decoy Despatch

And exactly according to programme, I fell in with General Putnam's outposts, when I was taken to the general himself, who chanced to be at that point. He had known me. Now I thought he would read my soul.

" You are turned honest, Philip ? "

" I always was," said I, bridling; and carrying on the show of the thing, I added, " but your excellency knows that I could not but hand you that despatch — although I was bribed to the contrary."

" You are one of the men who, God helping, will win this fight," the general continued. I could not face his simple directness. He added, " I 'll send it to General Washington."

Outside, where I went as free as the air, I sickened of it all. And then, in the village, I saw Peggy. What she was like I can't say, save that she was, and is, the girl for me.

When we had talked, I boasted :

The Decoy Despatch

" I have money, Peggy. Now we can be married."

" How did you come by it, John Philip ? "

I could lie glibly before General Putnam, but not before her eyes. I stammered.

" Had it anything to do with the despatch ? " said she, — " anything at all, John Philip ? "

" Yes," said I; and I could not lie to her, strangely enough. " Yes."

She drew back with horror on her face. " Talk not to me — spy ! " said she.

I thought she called to me, but I could not turn back.

Spy ! The word rang in my ears. Yes, I was, plainly enough. She was right. And suddenly I detested myself. I was traitor. I could not help being traitor to one or the other. But which ? I felt in my pocket, where the sovereigns jingled. One I took and flung far away from me. And then I paused, laughing.

The Decoy Despatch

'T was equally sin to throw away good money. I searched in the road for the piece. But it had gone, and then I sighed at my impulsiveness.

But there were other considerations than these of money in this affair. Clearly there was that of honor, which I had lost, whichever way I might turn. There was only one way, after all — I could not disguise it — and that was the way Peggy's scorn made imperative.

"I wish to see the general," I asked of General Putnam's orderly, and in a few minutes I was again in the general's presence. He regarded me with surprise, I think, which I understood only too well.

"What is it, Philip?"

"The letter?" said I, faintly.

"It's gone to General Washington," said he, his voice not unkind.

"General," said I, "that was a decoy letter."

"What d'ye mean, man?"

The Decoy Despatch

"It was intended to fall into your hands."

He looked as if he thought me mad.

"D'ye know that you risk death as a spy?"

"I know it," said I, and then I fumbled in my pocket and counted out the sovereigns. "These are properly yours. They gave them to me to carry the letter and to be arrested with it. One I threw away." For a moment he paused; for a moment looked me over from head to toe. "It's this," said I, answering his look in kind, and finding I could face him unflinchingly: "I'm a poor man, General Putnam. The money — and freedom — were temptation. I have been prisoner with them so long I wished freedom. I was tempted — thought I could carry this thing through. But I can't, General Putnam; I have told you everything."

I wondered what he would do then. I knew he was a decided man, to whom I could talk more easily than to some of the fine gentlemen in our service. I don't believe I should have had the heart before another; but to him it was different. He was more of our Northern farmer class — could feel my temptation.

Now he did a queer thing, for he advanced after looking me over narrowly.

"Philip, you have been tempted. I understand. I suspected the color of the despatch, which on its face was unreasonable. But I shall have to have you put under arrest. I'm sorry, man. But I honor your confession, — your attempt to atone for what you have done."

I bowed my head, for I could not answer. Again I was under arrest, and for the moment I regretted it, and then regret passed. The girl who had scorned me would hear of this. She would know that at least I had made a sacrifice to atone for what I had done. And then it seemed that my conscience approved. I had been unfaithful to my employer, Ratham; but I had turned over the money, my price, to

The Decoy Despatch

General Putnam. The general had not mentioned — simply had taken it. I supposed that it was contraband of war on my confession.

And here was I prisoner again, on my own confession, with death after the court martial before me. I could not imagine it turning out differently.

And so six days passed, and on the morning of the seventh the sentinel came.

" You are free, Philip."

" Free ? "

" Yes," said he; " here 's the order. The court martial decided your confession made up for your deed. You are dismissed the service."

I could not understand it as I stumbled out. Free! Could it be? But dismissed the service in dishonor!

Outside was the girl Peggy. Would she turn from me?

" John Philip," said she, and her voice was timid.

" Can you speak to me ? " said I.

146

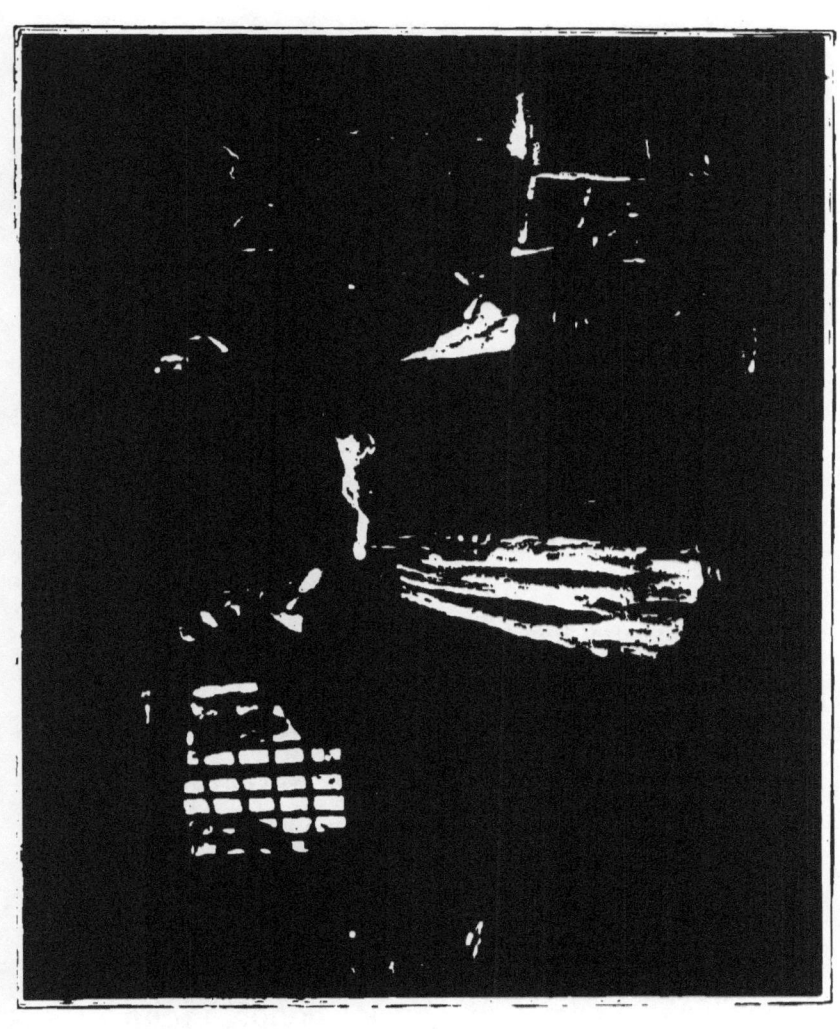

"You have won back honor, John Philip,—and me, if you will have me."

The Decoy Despatch

" Yes, John Philip."

" You forgive me ? "

But I had no need to ask.

" And General Putnam gave me this for you."

And she showed me a bag with the sovereigns Ratham had obtained for me from Sir William Howe — lacking the one.

" How did you know — " I began.

" I went to General Putnam," said she.

" You pleaded for me ? "

" Yes," said she, softly.

And then I took the bag of gold.

" I must return this to Ratham. I have not earned it."

" I like to hear you say that, John Philip."

" Oh, if I were not a dishonored man ! "

" You have won back honor, John Philip — and me, if you will have me."

" But — I cannot — " I began.

" You would not leave me unhappy ? " she began.

The Decoy Despatch

But I sent the gold to Ratham. The piece that was lacking I borrowed.

After a time came his answer: " Fool, you must have had a higher price."

I did, I am free to confess, — Peggy, and some approval of my own conscience, on a little farm in the Catskills. But among men I am known still as " Philip the spy," for such a thing you cannot live down.

But I have found that some self-approval and the approval of those you hold dearest are more than the world's. Still I was cowardly. My repute has been hard for her. For her I was selfish. And I believe now I have been punished, because it was really not so much my wish for self-approval that led to my confession as the wish for her.

And it's for my children, too, to bear. I wonder how God's way is? Yet I know I have not earned peace, because I should have borne my sin alone.

The Pretty Wit of
Captain Paul Jones

The Pretty Wit of Captain Paul Jones

MANY things are told of that redoubtable adventurer Paul Jones — whom I knew well — to concede him, with Mr. Jefferson and Dr. Franklin, the most supreme merit as a man of resource.

Made as he was with the tireless spirit of effort, it was to be expected that he should end as he did, disappointed in his career. I know of nothing sadder, more tragical, than the end of that poor chevalier of the Order of Merit of Louis XVI., who had been a most doughty captain in our navy, and an admiral among the Russians, where political intrigue obscured his ability, dying as he did in Paris in 1792. I like to think of him better as I knew him in the fame that the victory of the " Bon Homme Richard " over the " Serapis " had secured him, when he took on rather the manner of a beau, assumed fine airs, sported the sword the king had given him, was petted by the ladies, — even by Marie Antoinette, then in the fine heyday of her gayety before her sad end; I mean the time when he had his celebrated affair with la Comtesse de Bourbon, and with Madame Thellison.

For this little swarthy fellow, with his peering eye, his boasting over the greatness of the republic he served so well, was ever the admirer of a petticoat when its wearer was fair. I am told he had several duels on his hands on that account, of one of which and its mysterious cause Dr. Franklin himself has preserved the account.

But there is another, — one between himself and one of the fairest, cleverest, most charming and dangerous women of the court at Versailles, which I have never seen recorded, and which I will put down as I had it myself from the great captain's lips.

Captain Paul Jones

The lady was la Comtesse Hortense Le
Fevre, a rich young widow, and who, besides Captain Paul, had many aspirants to
her favor, among others Lord Whittlesey,
of the English foreign office.   In the end
she became, as you will remember, the
Countess of Whittlesey, the mother of the
present earl (1813).

Now, at that time, the English were
piqued at Captain Jones, would not allow
him any merits excepting of the Captain
Kidd order, and dearly wished to catch
him that they might swing him from a
yard-arm.

Well, Captain Jones, just then idle,
and because he was a man who must have
some activity, even if it were playing with
the fire of the devil, found time for many
affairs, as I have said.   Among others he
conceived the passion for Madame Le
Fevre.   She was of medium height, fair,
plump, with the most bewitching lips, and
enticing gray eyes, always exquisitely gowned
among Marie Antoinette's ladies, always

most proficient at the affected simplicity that played about The Little Trianon.

And behold our swarthy American captain, the great son of a Scotch gardener, sighing for her, until all the court noticed it, and made sport of him, and called him Madame la Comtesse's " Poor Paul." And madame herself liked it all, counting him but one more victim. But she played him off, as she did many other gentlemen, French, Italian, Germans, and Russians, who wrote verses to her and called her the fair cruel cold Le Fevre after the fashion of that day, when the sentimentality, as Monsieur Rousseau so well expressed it, but hid the horrid seriousness of the time under this veneer all " out of joint."

She smiled, as I say, on all; had no favorite; flirted and encouraged just enough without suffering scandal to touch her skirts. And in the mean time, though no one knew it, she had become secretly plighted to Lord Whittlesey. It would not have been prudent for a lady who courted popularity at Versailles at this period to have confessed a penchant for an Englishman.

Now, while our captain was a shrewd fellow on the quarter-deck, he was a simpleton where a woman was concerned, as many brave men before and since have been. More than simple, he was as vain as a peacock over his achievements in this direction.

And so one night, after a great affair at court, when madame la comtesse had been particularly cold, he was not surprised on returning to his lodging to find a pretty scented note on his table, in Madame Le Fevre's hand, by all the gods of love and war. He puffed up indeed after all the chargin of defeat. "You never can tell about a woman," he muttered. "When her manner is distant she sometimes likes you most." And with this trite reflection, which shows how silly a really brave man may be when out of his element, the doughty captain opened the note, which read : —

The Pretty Wit of

My dear Captain, — If you will be at nine o'clock to-morrow evening entirely alone at the house with the carved griffins on the Rue Richelieu you will learn that the admiration of a brave and famous sailor is appreciated. Raise the knocker three times in quick succession.

Hortense Le F.

For a moment, despite all his vanity about his achievements with the sex, Captain Jones wondered. Could it be true? But there was the note and her name.

If Captain Jones had been himself he never would have run into the snare. Yet possibly he was, after all, his simple, natural self, the gardener's son, not quite to the manner born, a bit too vain, too credulous of his possible achievements with great ladies.

The long next day lagged. He powdered his hair, and put on his gayest costume and the fine sword Louis XVI. had given him in compliment of the victory of "Le Bon Homme Richard;" then when

Captain Paul Jones

near the hour he sallied forth to keep the appointment, for he never doubted but that his charmer awaited him.

The house, a building of the Fourth Henry's time, he often had noticed; for with the curiously carved griffins at each side of the door, bearing the arms of a former prince of Condé, it was unmistakable.

Now, as he took his eager way through the darkening streets, he had no difficulty in finding it. The streets of Paris were not then as cleanly as they were to become in the great emperor's time; and the captain, who walked, as a matter of caution, was grieved to think that his shoes and stockings were mud spattered. He stood there for a moment, among the few passers, thinking ruefully that this was the case, and observing closely the shuttered front of the house. And then, although that silent, impassive front had made him a bit suspicious, he lifted the knocker once, twice, thrice, just at nine o'clock. A lover, like a warrior, should be exact in his appointments.

But was he not in fact ahead of the time? Was it only a trick? He started to lift the knocker again, when the heavy door swung open a crack and a wrinkled face peered over the chain.

"Captain Paul Jones?" queried an uncertain voice.

"Yes, I," assented Captain Jones, when the chain rattled, was loosed, the door swung open on a hall all dark, and the concierge, or whatever she was, motioned him in. The woman closed the door, leaving him in the blackness of the interior, now for the first time with the thought of the need of caution.

And as he thought of possibilities of danger after all the ardor of his hope, he was caught from behind by strong, invisible arms; a gag was passed over his face; and though he tried to struggle, and he was one of those little wiry men, it was all in vain. He was borne to the floor, bound, and his eyes bandaged, his assailants the meantime saying not a word.

The whole occurrence was uncanny, — this sudden attack in the obscurity of the house where he had expected light and laughter ; the strong men who mutely held him, and against whom any struggle was vain, — these circumstances left the Chevalier Paul Jones shivering, bound and gagged, and blindfolded as he was, and thrust aside in a corner, like a dead thing. And then, as he strained his ears, his hearing indeed being the only faculty of which these bravoes had left him the use, he heard doors shutting and the sound of heavy steps on the hard floors of deserted rooms. His reason began to return then, and the first thing that occurred to him was that his silent assailants had worn no shoes. Was this man or men different ? And then of course he perceived that, having accomplished the assault, need of silence no longer existed. That was patent. They had put on their shoes. But again the house grew still, excepting for his breathing.

His hands tied behind him and his feet together, with a strong rope that cut into the flesh — his eyes bandaged, his mouth gagged — finding struggling useless, and only knowing that the assailants had dropped him where they had taken him, our brave chevalier was indeed in a horrid predicament. The only thing he could do was to roll over the floor. He could do that with difficulty, and to and fro, right and left; and he began the examination of the room in that awkward manner, which was the only way that indeed was possible.

Rolling to his right about three feet, he brought up against a wall; to his left a distance of ten feet, he bumped his head, which the tortoise-like movement brought first against the wall. This was a hall, fourteen feet more or less broad. He judged the distance from the number of turns his body made, while he paused, breathing hard, as this effort, bound as he was, was most exhausting. If you do not believe me, have yourself bound tight, hands and feet, gagged, and eyes blind-folded, and then try to roll about.

As the Chevalier Jones lay there in this fashion, breathing hard, and his plight apparently hopeless enough, he thought in a revengeful spirit of Madame Le Fevre, who plainly had brought him into the plight. He remembered that two days after there was to be a great ball at Versailles, on which he had counted. He thought of the fine clothes he had worn to the appointment which were torn and hopelessly ruined. He thought of the sword the king had given him and which the assailants had taken away. And as he lay there his heart was bitter over the simplicity of the stratagem.

And what did they intend to do with him? For a moment he was cold with perspiration as he thought the men would return, carry him out, and perhaps drop

him into the Seine. Then he reflected
that if they had wanted to be rid of him
they would have killed him with a sword
or dagger thrust. More likely they wanted
to kidnap him. If they had wished to kill
him they certainly would have stabbed
him beyond any noise. But why should
they wish to kidnap him unless —

The plot suddenly became as clear as
day. They would carry him to the coast,
put him on some smuggler, and deliver
him to the authorities in England, who
had a large reward offered for his apprehension as a pirate dangerous to his majesty's shipping and coast. Had he not
himself abducted Lord Selkirk? And now
the same methods were tried on him,
the abductor. Madame Le Fevre plainly
had engaged some desperate fellows, of
whom Paris held many, who, having nothing to lose, gladly had embraced the chance
of obtaining the reward offered for the
apprehension of the " pirate Paul Jones."
They had caught him neatly, and now

they had gone after the carriage which was to carry him out of Paris.

Impatient and angered over his own simplicity in this matter, his wretched vanity about women, he began to struggle and roll about again. After he had struggled for some time vainly at his bonds, the spirit of investigation returned, and he began to roll over and over, now in the other direction of the room.

Counting the distance with the same method of calculating it he had used before, the length of that room seemed endless. He knew he must make considerable noise with his shuffling about in that house, which apparently was now deserted.

Pausing out of utter exhaustion and breathing hard, with the gag cutting into his mouth, he almost despaired. And then taking courage he again began to move about, when he thought his hands were not so much hindered. Certain, all at once, that the rope had stretched, he stopped his rolling and tried to move the arm that seemed to be least confined. As he did this the rope stretched further. With hope he worked at it again. These fellows were not sailors in the tying of a knot, God be thanked; and after a half hour in this struggle he was able to free a hand.

Now give a man like Captain Paul Jones one hand free and he could accomplish the rest. Twenty minutes after, he was on his feet, bruised and maimed between his struggles with his assailants and the scarcely less severe one with his bonds. But he was free again, clothes torn, himself cut and bruised, the ropes and bandages that had confined him in a heap on the floor.

The room was dark except for the light that entered from a high window in the rear.

And just then he heard steps as from some distant part of the house. Trying the front door, which had admitted him, he found it closed. In his desperation he turned through a door at the left, opposite to that from which the steps came. Seeing a window in this room, he sprang toward it, pushed it up, while over his shoulder a glare of light fell from the next room.

" Gone ! " cried a voice in consternation, and in English.

" The devil ! " exclaimed another in French.

" Quick, he is in the next room ! " said the first.

By this time Captain Jones had his window opened, and, without pausing to examine where he was to land, he was over the sill, while a bullet fired by one of the pursuers whistled past his ear. He heard the report an instant after he sunk on the soft turf. For, as luck would have it, — the luck which favors those men that dare all things, — he had fallen on the turf in the little garden back of this house. In the opened window above appeared suddenly two faces. There were two of them.

" Wretches," cried the Chevalier Jones, forgetting all prudence, " if I had known there were only two of you I had stopped to kill you."

For answer one of the fellows thrust his leg over the sill and dropped, with an oath, into the garden. Quicker than a flash, and not considering how many others might follow, Captain Jones's fingers, still numbed with the bands, were at his throat, while the other fellow paused in the window above, disregarding his comrade's plight, or doubtless thinking he should be able to settle a man weakened as Captain Paul Jones certainly must be after his terrible experience. At the moment a loud pounding was heard at the street door. The man in the window, knowing that this probably came from the watch aroused by the pistol shot, turned and fled from the window, doubtless considering it near impossible to get away over the high wall enclosing the garden, and knowing an exit in the rear.

Captain Jones, left with his man, and

being still on top in the struggle, clung to the fellow's throat with the tenacity of desperation, till the man sank back choked into unconsciousness.

The noise and cries at the front door still continued.

By this time the excitement of the little action had restored Captain Jones's sense. Kicking the fellow to find whether he was really unconscious, he looked up to see if he could not gain the house, to admit the people at the door, who, he thought, undoubtedly were the watch. Noticing a vine that crept up the stones almost to the sill, he found that clinging to it he could gain the sill.

A lantern was on the floor of the room, as the desperadoes had left it.

In the mean time the knock and voices at the door were imperative.

" Open, in the king's name ! "

" I cannot. They have taken the key."

" And who are you ? " demanded the voice, the knocks ceasing.

"The Chevalier Paul Jones, beguiled to this house and robbed."

"The Chevalier Jones!" exclaimed the voice, incredulously.

The chevalier, or better the captain, as his proudest American title was, was known and admired throughout Paris. The watch could not believe it was he. He insisted he was Captain Paul Jones. He told them to try the rear door, by which he believed one of the men had escaped. The house was on the corner of a lane turning from the Rue Richelieu into the adjoining street. The watch found easily an entrance by which the man in the house had escaped.

Captain Paul Jones now had no difficulty in proving his identity to the captain of the watch, who recognized, for all his bruises and torn and dirtied person, that this was really the redoubtable American sailor.

One man had fled certainly. The woman who had admitted Captain Jones was not to be found. The house had no furniture of any kind, and had been rented a week previously by an unknown man who had paid for six months in advance. In the garden the one fellow was found, just recovering consciousness, and recognized as a well-known Parisian desperado.

This fellow would give no explanation of the plot, though smartly questioned at his trial. Preserving that " honor among thieves " which proves that some robbers might have made, under other circumstances, excellent and honorable soldiers, he died on the gallows bravely without a word of confession.

Captain Paul Jones, now having quite recovered that pretty wit which had stood him in such good stead on many another occasion, drove at once to the minister, the Comte de Vergennes. Insistent on seeing him, he succeeded, and told the whole affair over, with his own belief that it had been a plot to abduct him and carry him to England. Monsieur de Vergennes concurred with him that the object of justice might be gained best by keeping the affair entirely private, at least for some days. He congratulated Captain Jones on having escaped as he did with only a few bruises. Captain Jones, on his part, said that he was glad that he had not suffered the loss of the sword the king had given him, which had been found in one of the rooms of the house.

When Monsieur de Vergennes questioned him narrowly about what had led to the appointment, he said he could not reveal the person's name. When Monsieur de Vergennes was insistent that the facts might be laid properly before the minister of police, Captain Jones was equally reticent. He could not tell.

" Ah, yes," acknowledged Monsieur de Vergennes, since he was of the ever gallant race; "I partly comprehend, and I suppose I cannot shake your obstinacy."

Monsieur de Vergennes could not; for Captain Paul Jones, though this woman certainly had tried to carry out the most hideous plot against him, did not consider it quite fair to punish her as if she were a man. Besides, he shrewdly guessed that she would swear that her name had been used without her knowledge, that the conspirators had simply played on Captain Jones' well-known vanity about women. Nor, indeed, as a matter of pride, did he care to have himself shown in the ridiculous light which a statement of the exact truth to Monsieur de Vergennes would put him.

But he had his own notion of a fine private revenge.

The next day no soul in Paris except his servant saw Captain Paul Jones. He told the servant to tell all callers that his master had gone away the previous evening without explanation, and had not returned. In the mean time he took needed rest — as much as he could in his meditation over revenge, and with the painful bruises he had received. One eye was black, and that side of his face badly swollen.

The next evening following was that of the great ball at Versailles I have mentioned. In the midst of the festivities who should appear with black eye and swollen face but this gardener's son of Arbigland in Kirkcudbrightshire, the famous knight of his most Christian majesty's Order of Merit, Captain Paul Jones.

Everybody smiled. Mr. Franklin, who was our minister then, looked grave. What ridiculous row had Captain Paul Jones been involved in now, to present so disreputable an appearance?

But though ladies tittered before whom earlier in the week he would have shone, our great captain had no vanity on this occasion. He had only eyes for Madame Le Fevre. In his pocket was the fatal note.

He was rewarded, nay, had almost positive proof. Madame Le Fevre nearly fainted when she saw him.

He walked straight to her, when she was by an evident effort recovering her self-possession.

" The heat here is oppressive, Captain Jones," she said.

"May I have a word with you, madame ? "

She scanned him closely. The little captain looked dangerous. Relying on her wiles, she thought it best to humor him, to cajole him out of his bad humor. Some beautiful women, in the conceit of a thousand successes, believe they can do anything they wish with men ; and was not woman the one vulnerable part in Captain Jones's armor?

So, now smiling, though she was fearful enough, she let him take her aside into one of the recessed windows looking out on the great fountains of the inner court of the palace.

" And what have you to say, chevalier ? " she began.

" To commiserate madame on her disappointment at finding I did not take a certain pleasant excursion to England."

Despite her knowledge of the great need

of keeping her self-control to meet him squarely, Madame Le Fevre trembled.

"Monsieur — " she began.

"I have your note," he began.

"My note! Give it me, monsieur! give it me, I pray! Surely you would not torture me so — you would — "

"Ah, madame," said Captain Jones, "you have confessed — and — I despise you — who — with all your charms, your greatness, your virtue, which I believe in, are yet more despicable than the poorest girl who passes on the street."

"You would not, monsieur?" cried the woman, in her desperation.

"Madame, if you appear at court after to-night, I will tell all. I swear I will tell all."

Madame Le Fevre began to weep.

Now, Captain Jones, in telling me this story himself, confessed that he never could withstand a woman's tears, and this woman, despicable as she was, yet had made him in love with her charms. So,

Captain Paul Jones

suddenly, impulsive as he was in such affairs, Captain Jones took the letter from his pocket, and tore it into pieces.

"Madame," said he, "I fight men — not women, though I confess they are vastly more dangerous. I believe it's a brave man's part to use no force against a woman enemy, but simply to despise her — to hold her less than the dirt under his feet."

And, turning on his heel, he left her.

In telling the story long after, Captain Jones said that no one in Paris ever had from him the true version of this adventure, and as I believe he esteemed it wrong, as he said, for a brave man to fight a woman, however dangerous she might be, I readily believed him.

NOTE. — The lady in the case afterwards married the Earl of Whittlesey, a circumstance which may explain her motive in the affair. Her son is that young Lord Whittlesey who lately distinguished himself in the Peninsular Campaign.

F. MIDDLETON, *Naples*, January, 1813.

The Meddling Hussy

The Meddling Hussy

I REMEMBER my man was smug-faced, appearing to all the world the reputable citizen, round, fat, a most politic and non-committal fellow, and I wondered whether I might not have gone wrong. But the direction was plain, " Philip Roland, Merchant, 5 Pearl Street, back of Fraunces's Tavern," and here was the man in his shop, looking at me narrowly over the gold rims of his spectacles. The Guards' Band was playing on the Bowling Green, for, though November, it was a warmish Indian summer evening, while he gloated over the letter, regarding me ever and anon in the dim light of the lantern that stood on the counter. He was a dealer in women's gewgaws, and esteemed as good an American as any man in New

The Meddling Hussy

York. I had heard, indeed, so much to this
effect that now I was uneasy to think perhaps I had but put my neck in the noose.
Had not the general been mistaken in the
man? Why did he pause so long? I
moved nervously, while before the window
passed some people returning from the play
at the Theatre Royal on John Street.

The royalist dandies had refitted that
little red theatre, closed by Congress with
a view to improving the public morals, and
plays had been writ for it by Major John
André. I shuddered as I thought of him,
for it was not so long since the scene at
Tappan; and, for all I had experienced in
the last days, causing me to regret my
mission, my softness hardened at that
name. As it happened, as if to empha-
size the thought, a link boy passed just
then before Mistress Susannah De Lancey
and Major Williams of the Artillery, who
had been André's intimate.

My *vis-à-vis* noted my uneasiness out
of his cunning eyes.

The Meddling Hussy

" There be spies and spics," said he. " But you, sir, surprise me. There lay every reason why you should return to the cause, and yet you risk your neck apparently as merrily as a boy after a bird's nest."

" Eh, yes," said I, gathering heart. " And I propose to have the bird to-night at eleven when he walks in the garden back from Burns's."

" Does he walk then in the garden ? " said he, peering at me.

" Yes, an uneasy conscience — "

" Ah, has he that ? "

" If he have not, my friend, I propose to make him uneasy, should you have your boat at the foot of the lane exact at eleven. I loosed part of the paling at the end of the garden, and there, behind the boards, which he now can wrench off in a trice, is Jem Hawkins. You know him ? "

" And you, sergeant ? " said he, curiously, and looking about lest the walls had ears.

181

The Meddling Hussy

" I, master, will stroll out of the tavern
as debonair as you please. I shall knock
our traitor over the head. Jem will break
through the paling, and we will carry him
to your boat."

" Should you be stopped ? "

" Humph, we have but to say we are
sailors from the ' Anne Marie ' taking a
drunken comrade aboard. Once in the
boat we shall pull for Hobock, where
Major Harry expects us."

I thought exultantly of this point in the
programme so well outlined, could it be
carried out; for it meant my restoration
to the old esteem among my comrades,
who now must be holding me the most
dastardly deserter.

" You have a glib tongue," my shop-
keeper said doubtfully when I had ended.

" It has persuaded Sir Henry, my old
friends, and their Brevet-Brigadier traitor
Arnold," I boasted; " now it wants but
your boat."

He reached forward, as if with enthusiasm out of keeping with the former suspicion.

"You risk death and so do I, should we be seen together. The boatman shall be there at eleven o'clock."

I was sure of him now, this person no one suspected, but who was one of those agents by whom Washington was kept conversant with occurrences in New York. I relied implicitly on the other man Hawkins, who was a hostler at "Fraunces's Tavern," for he had proven his honesty by seeing that my letter had reached the general, telling him exactly who had been implicated with Arnold in that damnable plot ; and now all that was left of the mission was to catch the traitor.

This was my fifth evening as an American deserter and king's man ; and it, I said, should not pass without me putting my hands on him for whose avarice André had suffered.

Yet, as I strode about the street corner past one of Mayor Matthew's watch, I

The Meddling Hussy

sickened of the attempt for the hundredth
time. I thought of how much they had
left me to do, how great a sacrifice of
good name I already had made, and how
little wit I, indeed, had to redeem it.

Before the ruins of Trinity Church,
standing out sepulchrally in the darkest
November night, I went in to sit on one
of the benches that had been built there at
General Pattison's suggestion, shortly after
the great fire; for the British policy was to
gain favor by making the town life agreeable
for those who could be caught by pleasure.

There in the dark I ran over the whole
unpromising phases of the enterprise: how
five days before, my commandant, Major
Lee, had summoned me to tell me that the
general had asked him for a man who
would dare risk everything to gain information of how the Arnold plot ran and of
those implicated; one who would even
dare kidnap the traitor in the very enjoy-
ment of his safety. The man who so
dared must appear to desert from Tappan.

The Meddling Hussy

This was asking much: my honor among my comrades and the risk of a spy's death from the British; and yet, young fool of twenty-three that I was, I accepted.

I can see that low room now, in the De Witt house in Tappan, the general's anxious face, Major Harry's bold eyes.

I turned my mare through the picket line and gave her free head when the patrol challenged, dashing over the moist roads, for, as bad luck would have it, the rain had blotted out the ruts, leaving the mare's footprints patent to the pursuers, for the farrier put the same mark on the left forward shoe of all Major Lee's horses.

For the moment, I believe, they hesitated, dumfounded that so faithful a soldier as I should suddenly imitate Arnold. In all the disaffection there never had been a desertion from that corps. Who can be trusted? I could fancy them muttering. I knew that Major Lee would delay them all he could; but he, too, must carry out the play. He, too, must appear astounded that I, who always had proven faithful, should all at once become among the most faithless. I thought all this while the mare bore me over the road toward Bergen, for I designed to hail the king's patrols at Paulus Hook.

But with all the delay I had but little the start. Soon I heard them after me, and the mare almost spent. The sky lightened. The mare seemed to be going even slower, and I knew as I came to the forks on the hill, which is by the " Three Pigeons" inn, above Bergen, that they probably would catch me before I could make the stone bridge below. Nay, turning in my saddle I could see in the darkish dawn Cornet Middleton heading the pursuers, and hear his loud hallo.

At the forks, within a stone's throw of the " Three Pigeons," for a moment I deliberated. Should I have my reputation all lost for nothing? They probably would shoot me as it was, nor could they ever believe me an honest man.

The Meddling Hussy

Only for a moment did I hesitate, you may believe, before turning directly down the slope by Elizabeth Point to the river, and there, as luck would have it, was a patrol. I sprang from the mare, and waded through the marsh into the river, hallooing. Just then the pursuers perceived my detour, and a bullet came singing around my ears. I pushed out beyond my depth, and the men in the boat, comprehending the situation, pulled me in, firing and shouting derisively to my old comrades, whose curses reached me.

I was taken to Sir Henry Clinton, who, examining me closely, ended by believing in my sincerity, as in faith the desertion was plain enough, and that one from Major Lee's corps.

As we had thought would be the case, he recommended me as an honest fellow to General Arnold, who, too, had run to the king's side. I could detect a certain detestation in Sir Henry's tone when he spoke of Arnold, who had received his

The Meddling Hussy

£10,000 and his Brigadiership as the price of his service, who yet was sincerely disliked, more because the affair had cost the army Major André, I believe, than for any other reason.

I reported that morning to the new British Brevet Brigadier, at 3 Broadway, in the old ball rooms over " Burns's Arms."

I do not know what I had expected of the man. I had heard so much to his discredit. I saw an agreeably mannered gentleman, who questioned me closely, and in the end believed that I had been persuaded by his example.

Strangely, too, he rented of a widow, Mistress Warren, whose daughter, Priscilla Warren, I once had made furious love to in Virginia. A plump, fair-haired, gray-eyed girl, Mistress Priscilla's greeting, her congratulations to me at having come over from rebellion to loyalty, made me for a moment sicken again of my part.

I must explain this to show how that

which followed came about. Nor did Benedict Arnold fail to treat me with further consideration. He promised to obtain me a commission in a legion of American loyalists in time to join the expedition Lord Howe was then preparing to send to the Virginia capes. In the mean time, other decent lodging being hard to find, he had permitted me to take a room at the Widow Warren's.

In fact, all had gone exactly as the plan had been laid. I had communicated, as I have said, with General Washington, showing him, as I had it from Arnold himself, who appeared to trust me implicitly, the full extent of the treachery, and the names of the few persons in any way implicated. I have been told that this information first gave the general-in-chief heart to believe there remained those he could trust; and that the major-general he suspected was, after all, not in the affair.

And now the rest was all plain. Arnold

would stroll in the garden to quiet his
nerves before bed. My desperate fellow
would hide behind the loosed paling, I
could be sure, at the appointed hour. I
was now equally sure of Master Roland
having the boat in readiness at the foot of
the lane. Yet, as I thought of it all, I
felt dismayed. I looked up to the ruined
tower of Trinity, almost praying to keep
my courage warm. I decided to take a
tankard of beer at the tavern. The night
was dark enough, and now began a cold
drizzle. Long since the Guards' band
had stopped on the Green. What could
be better than such a night, made for the
adventure?

At last the clock ticked near the time
when General Arnold would descend for
his stroll in the garden. Even now I knew
my man Hawkins was waiting in the lane.
I paid my reckoning and turned for a moment into the street.

The mist was clearing. Certainly
General Arnold would take that walk to

get some air before sleep. But if he kept to his usual custom it lacked a half hour of the time. To avoid possible suspicion I turned into the tavern and up the stairs to my room. I intended to follow the general by the back stair. It all would be easy should he once go into the garden.

But at the head of the stair stood my acquaintance, Mistress Priscilla Warren, of whose mother General Arnold rented. She held a candle, as if expectantly, and I am bound to say she made a pretty picture at the stair head. I recollected how years before in Virginia I once had made furious love to this very girl.

"Jack! Jack Champe!"

"Eh, Priscilla. And why, mistress, are you not in bed?"

"The truth is," said she, blushing, "I've been thinking and pondering."

"Of a lover?" said I, trying to phrase some pleasing, nonsensical gallantry.

"Not I, sir, of no man but of you."

"Of me, Priscilla?"

The Meddling Hussy

" Ah, of you, who have made the whole town believe in you; but me — not a whit."

" And why ? " said I, growing impatient, for I heard General Arnold's step. " I must speak to the general, begging your pardon."

" Why ? " she asked, putting the candle close to my face. " Liar, you are not what you seem ! " Her voice had changed so suddenly that I lost my wit.

" Priscilla ! "

" You never deserted General Washington."

" Mistress Priscilla ! "

" You are here a spy — to betray General Arnold."

" Ah, mistress, but he is worse," said I, with sudden earnestness.

" He has treated you kindly, John Champe."

" You have the fancy of a silly maid ! " cried I. " Let me go. I must follow General Arnold into the garden."

Again she raised the candle a bit.   From below was the fiddler's merry jig.

" Why ? "

I trembled under those gray, questioning eyes, and she read my plot as easily as I had told her.   It all had gone well up to this moment.   My man was behind the paling.   The boat waited.   Colonel Lee across the river expected us.   And here this girl had in some way found the intention.

" I will explain later.   Now — "

She put the candle on the table.

" I will go with you into the garden."

" And why, unasked ? " said I, trying to treat the matter lightly.

At this she pulled from her bosom a letter in Major Harry's own hand, with the damning evidence.   She had me in her power as neatly as she could wish.   I had dropped it somewhere in the house.   Cursing my carelessness, I snatched at it, when she thrust it behind her.

" Spy ! " she said, as if I were less than the boards under her feet.

13   193

The Meddling Hussy

" And he ? " said I, doggedly.

" But does it lessen your blackness, coward, — you who return to your friends pretending you are converted to the old opinions, only to spy ? "

" Give me up, then," said I at last, defiantly. " Give me up."

" I will not tell a soul," said the girl at this.

" How could it profit you ? " asked I, trying to pacify her.

" Nor shall I let you hurt a hair of General Arnold's head — neither one nor the other."

She stood there, her hands thrust behind her. Suddenly the fiddler below paused in his air and left us in silence.

I must not let the pretty little fool thwart me when I had risked so much. No, she should not. The general was in the garden ; my man Hawkins was breathing hard behind the paling, waiting the signal. Every moment was dear.

" He may be traitor, but he has been

kind to my mother and to me," she went on. "You shall not hurt him. If he be traitor, was he not before one — to the king? Consider that."

I did not answer, revolving the problem how to get her out of the way, cursing my bad luck indeed in having dropped the luckless letter I should have burned.

"And why," she went on, taking a step nearer, "should you, Jack Champe, take further risk? You are back, without odium, in the king's service. You have but to forget your purpose, which was traitorous. You have before you a finer career than the rebels can offer."

And while we disputed by the candle-light Jem Hawkins behind the paling was wondering at the lack of the signal.

"I am pledged to Washington, I am with the United States," said I, desiring to be rid of her.

"And you are here as a spy?" she cried again, her gray eyes flashing.

The Meddling Hussy

" For all 's fair in war," said I, watching her that I might spring past.

" And in love," said she, blushing I thought, and wondered if she loved not Benedict Arnold, whom I began to hate with fierceness.

" But wait," said I, " Mistress Priscilla. I have a word to say to the general now in the garden. Surely there can lie no harm in that ? "

" Ah, I know you," she answered at this defiantly. " You have some design. I 'll accompany you."

By this time I was maddened. Have I not said how much every moment counted ? A bold move would accomplish it still. I was not to be foiled by this hussy.

So I pushed her aside, went through the door into the back hall, and down the steps leading to the garden.

There he was, pacing restlessly to and fro. Ah, the man never had a quiet moment between his plots and his re-morse, — for I believe he had that. Jem

The Meddling Hussy

Hawkins, I was certain, was waiting. I could carry it out yet.

But the girl was behind me, like a dog. I was sorry for a moment I had not throttled her.

"General Arnold!" she called from the foot of the stair. "General Arnold!"

Before I could get to him, he walked too far toward the house. In an instant he was by her. I saw she whispered something to him. Was it my betrayal?

For a moment I hesitated. I still could run for it; but should I escape, which was doubtful, it would be without my prisoner. For the moment she had foiled me. I must brazen it out, deny her charge.

So I returned to the upper hall, where they were talking. She looked at me, not triumphantly. I was surprised how pale he was.

"Sergeant Champe wished a word with you, sir," she said, without facing me.

How could I explain? I thought at

once of some story connected with the duty he had given me; but he anticipated me, saying: "I am too weary. Wait till morning. You will receive your regular duty then. Good night."

He extended his hand gravely, as if treachery had made us equals, and walked to his room. Outside, perhaps, Hawkins still waited. But the chance was lost for the night. The girl had outwitted me. Why had I not killed her?

As he left us alone she understood my rage, for she said quietly, "I did it to save you."

"You have not told him?"

"Not a word; you can still serve the king."

"Fool!" I muttered, as people do when only they are the fools. I heard her sobs and hurried from her, fearful what she might tempt me to.

Nor could I sleep. I dared not send word to Hawkins, or to the boatman at the end of the lane. Across the river at

The Meddling Hussy

Hobock Colonel Harry waited vainly. Because of this girl I was still held a traitor by my comrades; and it appeared, indeed, as if they must so regard me till the end of the chapter. For as I tossed restlessly, while it was yet pitch dark, there was a knock at the door, and the orderly shouting, "Up, sergeant, in a hurry. You have duty. The general's expedition pulls anchor at five for the Virginia capes!"

I saw beyond peradventure then that I had failed dismally. I should have no other chance at my man now, while if I wished to avoid the spy's death, I must keep up appearance and serve as a British soldier.

Outside in the hall was the girl, her eyes red by the candlelight.

"Forgive me!" said she. When I was silent she added, "I did it for you."

"For him."

"For you! To save you for the cause."

The Meddling Hussy

"Faugh," said I; "I despise you for a meddling hussy."

Yet I thought afterward she indeed had not betrayed me. That was certain. I wondered what was the reason, dismayed over the turn of the adventure.

For here was I, now bound for Virginia, as earnest a patriot as ever served in the war, but in the uniform of an English soldier, and commanded by the very Arnold whom I had come to take.

In addition the weather turned dirty, and I suffered the worst torments the sea can inflict on those so indiscreet as to trust to its fickleness. Let them be sailors who will, I would be content to be the humblest land lubber rather than to own all the fame of the most esteemed admiral.

I remember it was a week after we had made a landing before I recovered my heart and was in some way able to debate the chance of escape to the American lines. I had become, with memory of that wretched, discovered letter, as cunning as a fox. But, despite all my cunning, the chance never presented itself. I could not hope to abduct General Arnold, with no man whom I dared trust with even a hint of my true mission. How quickly I should be worsted !

Strangely, I did in my false position singularly good service. I was commended again and again when least of all did I want praise for a part I detested. That old saying of the mockery in the way of the world came to me in those days : " When you may be indifferent to success, lo ! it comes to you."

As a matter of fact, we remained in this inaction some three months, till we joined Lord Cornwallis at Petersburg. I then was detailed to go with a division instructed to intercept some reported foragers sent out by Major Harry Lee.

I strained my ears as I heard. I was arrayed against Major Harry, whom I loved, if I ever loved a man, both for being most considerate of his inferiors,

The Meddling Hussy

and always the dare-devil. I laughed as I thought of it — I against Major Harry!

Yet it was not so comical an affair in very earnest. Here in Virginia I was known. One day an old woman who had heard my history spat at me. I could not blame her.

But two persons I hated, Benedict Arnold and the meddling hussy. I thought I might kill him, and so, although I should certainly be hanged, I should be lauded by my old comrades as a hero, after all these days of apparently deserved contempt.

And yet I could not find courage for this. He had treated me from the first most considerately. I could not stab, or shoot behind his back. My instructions, in fact, had been to bring him in alive, not dead.

I thought, perhaps, of the meddling hussy at the stair head. She had foiled me, but, in some curious way, she equally had made it impossible for me to kill the man, had I the chance.

The Meddling Hussy

With all these conflicting notions, in the service where I appeared what I was not, what more natural than that I should try a foolhardy escape to the old lines I had deserted.

It happened one evening at a point near the Carolina line, when on that expedition I have described.

I broke away, much as I had at Tappan; but this time, knowing the country better than my pursuers, I managed to elude them with less danger to my skin.

As I was now walking my horse in the direction of the Congaree, where I supposed Major Harry to have been, I stumbled directly on one of his pickets. The man brought me in, covering me with his musket. And then suddenly he recognized me.

"Sergeant-Major Champe, the deserter!" he cried, at first incredulously, and again exultantly. "What a bird I have brought down!"

Others by this time had gathered; and

203

then an officer, before whom a black carried a lantern, approached over the halffrozen ground. It was early March.

"Major Lee!" I said, for by some chance I had fallen in with no less a personage. "Major Lee!" (He was then Lieutenant-Colonel of the Dragoons, though always "major" to me.)

"Where are you?" he began; and then, leaping from his horse, he cried, seizing my hands, —

"Champe!"

"Champe who failed!" I nodded, shamefaced. The men stood about astounded. For was I not a deserter? The major knew their thoughts.

"Sergeant-Major John Champe is this gentleman, who, like Captain Hale, to serve his country took on the disguise of a spy among the British."

When suddenly through that little detachment of my old comrades a cheer went up, and I believe that, after all I had imagined and suffered, this scene in the

The Meddling Hussy

Carolina swamp was the happiest of my life.

" But how did you fail, man ? " the major asked, when we rode to his main division. " I really believed you would carry it out. We waited at Hobock until too late for any possible hope of your appearance."

" Because of a meddling hussy," I said, my heart bitter against her.

" A wench ? I thought not that of you."

" Eh, but you must," said I ; and I told him the story.

" It is strange," said he, " why she did n't betray you. I can't understand it unless — "

" Unless ? "

" Unless she were in love with you," said Major Lee.

" Impossible," said I, forgetting to laugh. Why, of course it was absurd, although I could not get the notion out of my head.

At his headquarters, where my old comrades, who now knew the whole story, made much of my deed, although in faith it was failure enough, the major told me he could not take me back into my old company.

"And why?" I asked hotly, for I thought he meant that my failure to capture Arnold had discredited me with him.

" Because, Champe, I like you too well to have you risk capture by the British, who, before the clock could tick, would hang you as a spy."

I told him I cared not a whit for the danger; that I wanted to fight with all the strength and wit I had left after the false part I had played.

"Poor Champe," said he. " How badly have we treated you! But after all you have done I will not suffer you to risk a hair," he repeated.

When I was insistent he said finally that he had no option, but would refer the matter to General Washington, to whom directly I was despatched by General Greene.

I confess I was anxious when I came into the presence of that Virginia gentleman, who now had become the greatest among the Americans.

"You did us a signal service, Captain Champe," he said kindly, "in letting me know the extent of Arnold's treachery when I was uncertain of every one about me, and it must appear ungracious of me to tell you that out of regard for you and your most excellently good service, I must retire you — but as a captain, with a full captain's pay."

I did not want retirement. I cared not for the new grade, nor the money, though it was a scarce enough commodity in those days.

But the general was insistent. And in this way I ceased to be an active member of the army of the United States. In my forced retirement I was advanced in rank, yet a captain without hope of further ser-

The Meddling Hussy

vice, at least against the British, whom I
dearly wanted to fight in some capacity, —
a captain without a company.

Now about this time I had a strange
letter brought through the lines from New
York, and written by no less a person than
she who had spoiled my enterprise, Mistress Priscilla Warren. She begged me
never to give the British the chance of
catching me, for, as surely as her name
was Priscilla, they would hang me up as a
spy. I wrote her I had been told that
several times ; but I feared the British no
more than I did meddling Tory maids.

The hussy's impudence was strange.
But for her meddling I certainly had had
my plan to seize General Arnold carried
out. As it was, because General Washington was insistent on my retirement, and as
I had failed most dismally in this attempt, I
had not its success to console me for the
loss of the soldier's career I loved. I had
staked all, like a gambler, on one issue and
lost.

The Meddling Hussy

But I could not get the meddling girl out of mind, and thinking over the matter and considering that perhaps after all she had imagined it for my good — as possibly it would have been from a worldly point of view, — to have remained, what I seemed then, a British soldier, — thinking of the possibility of Major Lee's conjecture about the reason for her curious conduct, I resolved to see her again.

But it was not until after the peace that I had the chance, when, hearing she remained a spinster, I decided to leave Kentucky, where I had taken up some land, to see what manner of woman she had become.

I must acknowledge in the few years she had faded, and yet I found her strangely attractive. She appeared embarrassed at seeing me.

" You must detest me above all the rest of the world," said she.

" I did," said I, frankly.

The Meddling Hussy

"You did?" asked she.

"I don't now, Mistress Priscilla, for I believe you honestly imagined by meddling you could keep me a king's man. In the event it might have been better. I might have been richer."

"Yes," said she. "I think I even was right, Jack Champe."

"I am not accustomed, Mistress Priscilla, to women who will take the trouble you did to set a man right, although it was, from the point of honor, a wrong course, which I could not adopt. I believe you thought it for my good."

"There be many women who would have done so much," said she.

But I was firmly persuaded there was and is but one; and holding this persuasion and believing that now she might have me, although before, when, a boy, I had made violent love to her in Virginia she had jilted me, — believing that being a spinster now rather well along she might not refuse me, although, in faith, I had little enough money, I was persuaded to ask her to marry me.

" Me, Captain Champe! Are you not crazy? " said she, demurely, at this request of mine.

" Not I, Mistress Priscilla. I have a neat enough wit left to know the material for a good wife."

" Oh, but, captain, I 'm so old and ugly. Why did you not ask me when I was young? "

" I did when we were both young, years since, in Virginia."

" Oh, I forgot," said she.

" I tried then, but you jilted me; have you forgot? I supposed a woman never forgot whom she jilts."

" Oh, do you, captain? Or whom — "

" Or whom, mistress? "

" Or whom she loves? "

" Oh, then," said I, " I might as well return to Kentucky, for I see the jig is up."

" Is it? " said she. " I believe I even will go with you, captain."

The Meddling Hussy

" Are you jesting again, as you did when a girl in Virginia ? " asked I, doubting her.

" Eh, jesting, Captain Champe, as a spinster may who catches at perhaps her last and, indeed, I believe, her best chance."

I confess the outcome of the matter was most curious, for during those days when I was tossing on the sea on the journey to the Virginian capes, I should have held him as mad as the maddest March hare who had told me I should try to marry this meddling hussy to gain peace of mind.

But if the ways of God be strange, that way of His which is called woman's is the strangest. If any one were to blame for this termination of the affair of the meddling hussy, surely it was none other than Major Lee, who first had suggested to me an apparently impossible reason for her conduct when she had spoiled all my plan for catching the traitor. From regarding the reason all impossible, I began to ques-

The Meddling Hussy

tion if after all there might be some ground for holding it possible. The step from supposition to experiment is not a long one, as Dr. Franklin himself has attested. Yet I must confess I thought I was only a silly, imaginative fool for my pains, till her words showed that, strange as it may appear, Major Lee had understood her without ever having seen her.

Nor, in the end, although I have blamed her in all this account for having spoiled for me the outcome of a good adventure, was I so unfortunate as I had supposed. For if I did lose chance of further distinction as a soldier through following out the plan General Washington proposed to me, I learned in the end by this very adventure that a woman who takes enough interest in you to meddle with your matters, even to the point of turning them all topsy-turvy, may make, for the very reason of that interest, not so bad a wife.

Part II
Tales of Personages

215

The Loyalty of William Douglas

The Loyalty of William Douglas

I

WHEN William Douglas, the dissenter, came to Loch Leven, in answer to his aunt, Lady Douglas's summons, he held the Lady of the Scots, the Romanist, a wanton.

Yet for all that the Queen of the Scots had forfeited her sovereignty, and was the instrument of Romanish intrigue against the peace of Scotland, he felt a certain awe when he first accompanied Ferguson, the keeper, to do his cousin George Douglas's office as page before her.

Was not a princess different from other folk, and this one, an enticing witch? But with family pride strong in his heart, and with shame over his cousin's weak-

ness, he was determined not to be be-
witched.

The keys creaked in the great door
while Ferguson whispered under his breath :

" Beware, Master Douglas, and be
strong in the Lord. If she were queen
once, she ever was the wicked woman.
The blood of those her arts have slain
calls out on her."

She was by the window, where, at her
feet, her companion, Mistress Seton, was
reading in the French tongue. Her hands
supported her chin, and her eyes were
toward the free sky. Her face, thin and
worn, was framed by lightish brown hair,
that morning braided carelessly in long
folds over her shoulders. The hazel eyes
seemed to hold ready hate or love or
indifference. Douglas was to see this
charming face flushing with excitement;
now exquisite fair, it was of clear pallor
and the eyes underlined with a dark pen-
cilling. Her figure was daintily moulded,
and showed its slender proportions, through

the folds of the gown, which was of some gray stuff, plainly made. She wore no jewels, save a single ruby on a ribbon at her throat. A pretty lady, like any other, the young gentleman decided, and yet, decisions sometimes changing so rapidly where women are concerned, he put that away, and thought she was more.

When rising with a yawn she faced them, he saw she was of medium height, and looked gracious and amiable, with a manner that had exactly the right degree of unconscious familiarity with inferiors, yet could not forget she was some great lady. If under her eyes were bluish pencillings, and on her face the least suggestion of lines, she still had a certain girlishness which her voice confirmed, — a woman's voice with a maiden's quality. She looked the lady that might be sad in the morning, with the old zest of gayety by noon. He felt she was noting him carefully, and under her lashes was seeing him all, body and soul. He thought of what the preachers of Knox's following declared her — " Jezebel; " " the heathenish creature; " " a siren ! "

Yet after his second visit in the duty of page, he began to say to himself, " Surely, she is a pleasant lady who has been much belied."

But there were other moods, when she paced the room's length, no longer a charming gentlewoman, with the courtesies of the court, but more some caged tigress, ready, if the bars were but down, to rend and tear, looking cravingly into the open, out of her window, where birds and men seemed to her to do as they listed. Then, sometimes, keeper and page did not see her at all, only heard from the next room sobs, when Mistress Seton or Mistress Jane Kennedy would very civilly dismiss them.

Yet perhaps at breakfast the morning after, the queen would appear with a laughter-filled face, although her eyes might be hollow, and her gayety suggested the effort to force forgetfulness.

The Loyalty of William Douglas

And in this wise did Master William Douglas come to know and think differently of this princess, never seeing her alone, scarce noticed by her or her ladies, and always under the keeper's eye. But he carried thought of her to his sport with the men at arms, or to the hours he had in a skiff on the lake, or to the castle chaplain who told his congregation again and again the tale of the complete wickedness of mankind, the dreariness of this life, the flames and the devils that await us in the more painful future.

Now about this time the queen attempted to escape by donning the garments of the laundress who brought her linen from the village.

William Douglas, on the castle terrace that afternoon training a falcon, heard below the keeper's gruff cry, — " A too neat ankled laundress by half! " for though closely muffled, Mary Stuart's foot had betrayed her. Yet for all her disappointment at failure, and the sarcastic gibes

The Loyalty of William Douglas

Lady Douglas cast at her then, the dejected prisoner carried herself with the simple dignity the Stuart princess always had in face of adversity. No circumstances did so much to change William Douglas entirely to her cause as this adventure. Hardly more than lad, the queen may have read it in his eyes. Did she, she appeared to be looking beyond him, or to notice him no more than the stone blocks of the flooring. Nor did her ladies, who before, having no one else, had thought him worth an occasional smile, now seem to be aware of his presence. Finally he found their conduct, and particularly that of the queen, almost unendurable, although it was natural enough. He was decided to drop a note into the queen's lap as he passed, but that was too risky, and might only lead to his being removed from his post. Thinking over the riddle, at last one object came to have a fascination, its possession dearer than ambition or love or fortune, — that, the key-

The Loyalty of William Douglas

ring Master Ferguson had at his girdle;
and then our young gentleman of the
Douglases began almost unconsciously to
curry favor with the keeper: tried the art
of a player; maligned the queen, to the
keeper's delight, while inwardly cursing
him; used the canting phrases Scot dissenters affected, and slily discussed theology, which was a common topic.

But always those keys were in their
place at the keeper's girdle, unless he
should knife him behind.

Following out this wish to be near the
keys, he sat talking one night until near
ten o'clock with this Irish-Scot keeper,
who was expounding some theological
point, Douglas agreeing with him, the
time devouring with his eyes the bunch
of keys. A windy night it was of scurrying clouds, through which the moon would
break, sending an occasional shine across
the guard-room floor.

At last the keeper became drowsy, declaring he would go to bed.

15   225

The Loyalty of William Douglas

" But I could show this more clearly to you, Master Douglas, if I had my copy of Knox's sermons."

" If you 'll suffer me, I will go to your chamber with you, Master Ferguson, and bring the book that I may con the point."

" That you may, Master Douglas."

So he followed him out of the guard-room to the door of his chamber, that the keeper threw open, putting the lantern he carried on the floor, while he fumbled for the book. The gleam from the candle was shot back to the youth's eyes by the flaming key-ring. The pistol in Ferguson's belt caught him under the belly, and rising, he pulled it out, placing it on the board above the fireplace. With sudden impulse Douglas reached toward it; but turning, he slammed the door, that made clamorous echo.

" Eh, what 's that, Master Douglas ? " said the keeper, the book of John Knox in his hand.

The Loyalty of William Douglas

" The wind, Master Ferguson, the wind, I declare."

Leaping forward, he grasped the pistol from the board above the fireplace and faced the other.

" If it please you, Master Ferguson, the castle keys ? "

There was no premeditation. He had not dreamed of such an action. Its foolhardiness would have dismayed him. The keys, the mad desire to have them, possessed him like one of the devils Christ cast out.

Never was man more dumfounded.

" Are ye mad ? " he gasped.

" The keys, sirrah ! " said Douglas.

At this Ferguson muttered, " 'T is Jezebel's arts," and so exclaimed. With a blow he sent the pistol flying from Douglas's hand, caught him by the back, casting him with one thrust into the corner. The pistol, by fortune's power, was not discharged. The thick walls, the closed door, kept the scuffle unheard. Ferguson gazed at him in a heap in the corner, as he might be some worm.

"'T is you, master, following George Douglas's way. But you 're a madman."

He spoke sense. Douglas had yielded his secret. His plight could not be worse. A frenzy of unreasoned rage possessed him, and Ferguson's contempt gave a chance.

He knew not how suddenly he was on his feet, how he had sprung on the man, bearing him to the floor and choking him. The fellow could not cry out; his eyes, staring Douglas in the face, seemed to start from their sockets, while his face blackened in the lantern light. Had he choked him to death? He did not pause to query, but, relaxing his grasp, loosed the bunch of keys. As they fell rattling on the floor, Ferguson groaned, moving convulsively. Quickly Douglas undid his girdle, passed it through his mouth, and gagged him beyond sound. Seizing a deerskin from the bed, he cut it into thongs with the hunting-knife. With one thong he bound his hands behind his back, with the other tied his feet. At the moment his eyes opened. He had not choked his breath entirely out of him. " Thank the God of the Pope and of Knox alike," Douglas muttered.

" I 've the keys, old psalm-singer," said he. " Don't stare at me or struggle. My plight is desperate; I must free the queen, or die for it. Farewell, Master Ferguson."

Ferguson's eyes glowed desperation. Douglas wondered for a moment how his frenzy had the sense to choke him. By no other way could he have kept him from outcry, or, indeed, mastered him. If he had waited for a plan, he never should have done what he did. Ferguson rolled about the floor, making the moan of pain-bearing despair.

Taking the keys, Master Douglas picked up the lantern with the other hand, opened the door, closed and locked it, and dropping the keys in his pocket, strode down

The Loyalty of William Douglas

the corridor into the great hall. Instead of turning to his chamber, he opened the door to the corridor of the North Tower. Something like the frenzy poets tell of seemed to guide. He closed this door behind, locked it, and followed the narrow passage to the farther entrance, where the sentinel, who 'd been sleeping on the floor, sprang up, with staring eyes and gasping voice.

"Sleeping, honest Jock?"

"Not I, master. You saw not aright."

"I 'm not blind."

"A man may grow weary, master."

"He may get a dozen lashes."

"Ay, master, but you 'll not tell."

"It 's my duty. But I 'll try to forget.

"I came from Master Ferguson by my Lady Douglas's order, to carry a drug to the queen, who is ill. The apothecary but now brought it from the village."

In evidence of authority, he displayed the keys, at which Jock gazed in doltish amazement. Pushing him aside, Douglas unlocked the door.

"Now do you remain here by the open door, while I ascend the tower to the queen's apartment. No one can pass you."

"Not a soul, master," said he, as if reassured.

Lantern in hand, he went up the stairs to the door of the apartment, which he unlocked, closing the outer and knocking at the inner door. Again he knocked. At last, after a space, was Seton's voice:

"Who may be there at this hour?"

"I, mistress, — Will Douglas."

"You, master? What want you?"

"Word with the queen."

"Her Majesty has retired."

"I must see her."

"What mean you?"

"God help us! Ask not my meaning, but wake her!"

"Master, what treachery is this? I'll not open."

"Then, mistress, you waste my life."

The Loyalty of William Douglas

He heard the queen interrupting : —

" What's this, Seton ? "

" I don't comprehend, your Majesty, what treachery they now are at."

Douglas whispered through the keyhole : " Oh, your Grace, I'm here to free you. I've gagged and bound the keeper and stolen his keys. We have but a moment to try for the open. If we are caught, I shall be killed, and you ! I beg, your Grace, hasten ! "

" Wait ! "

He counted the moments until the door opened, and the queen and her lady were in the outer room. Her gown was hastily thrown on.

" Forgive me, Master Douglas, I thought you but a silly boy — Seton, a cloak ! "

" But I remain ! " said Mistress Seton.

" I'll not leave you ! "

" You must, your Grace. They cannot hurt me. If I stay I can pretend when they search that you are in the inner room."

The Loyalty of William Douglas

" They 'll believe it. I like your wit, mistress," said Douglas.

" That she has wit, Master Douglas, I know; that you had such readiness, I never suspected. Forgive me! I shall reward you if I escape. God forbid that an interest in my fortune may curse you, too. I hate to leave you, Seton."

" It 's better so," said the other.

For a moment the queen bent her head on her companion's shoulder, and, suddenly raising her face, she kissed her lightly.

" On, Master Douglas," said the queen's lady then. " You 're no boy, but a man after my heart."

" I have one to settle below, mistress," said he, noting her in the candle glare.

Closing the outer door, the queen came after. Half-way on the stair, he stopped her, while walking down, as if with great boldness, he threw back the door below.

" Jock," to the guard.

He closed the door, lest Jock should see the queen, and put the key in the lock.

The Loyalty of William Douglas

" I have delivered the drug."

" Yes, master. But is it not strange that Master Ferguson came not himself ? "

" Strange it is," said Douglas, fumbling at the lock. " This key will not turn. Will you try it, Jock ? The jamb is rusted, I deem."

" Yes, master."

As he turned to the lock, Douglas put the lantern on the floor, and whipping out his knife from the scabbard, and with a strong blow, thrust him through the back. With a groan the fellow fell over, while a stream of blood burst over Douglas's hand. The man's distorted face came before him afterward o' nights. But he had no other way, and it was the queen's cause.

The door was pushed back, and she stood there, the cloak on her arm.

" Are you hurt ? "

Douglas thought she would faint.

" The blood ! — the fearful blood ! — Not the first that 's been shed for me !"

The Loyalty of William Douglas

" Your Grace."

" I 'm cold."

Poor Jock lay in a heap on the floor,
his life blood still spurting. Douglas took
the mantle from the queen, and wrapt it
around her.

" Mind him not."

He tried to support her; for now he
was resolved they should get away.

" No, Douglas, I can walk as easily as
you for freedom's sake. But the poor
wretch, — he brings so many memories."

She seemed to sob, and to control herself, for her voice became dry and hard.

" We 'll go, master. Lead on."

He knew the way. Had he not studied
every turn during the weeks, when seeking
a means of aiding her, — every nook and
cranny?

So he led as easily as it were day, down
the passage to the great hall, where he
opened the door, which creaked on its
hinges. He dared not close it behind, but
went on, the narrow slits of the walls

The Loyalty of William Douglas

guiding. The door to the corridor of the postern-gate, he opened more carefully. It did not creak as the other. He took the queen's hand lest she should stumble.

The place was as still as the death he had wrought in the passage to the North Tower. But at the gate he was made to pause, having left the keys in the door to the Tower. Under his breath, he cursed. And here the queen, in that moment of perilous waiting, showed the Stuart spirit.

"But no blood, Douglas, even though they take us," she added, as she bade him take that dangerous walk back. In the passage was the gleam of the lantern, and the dead man in his blood. How grisly he seemed; how he mocked him! — he with whom he oft had laughed. And now never another stupid jest from the doltish brain. And he'd killed him! But — he had the keys at last. He must get away from that thing, the jeering, bloody face. Back he stirred.

The Loyalty of William Douglas

At the door to the hall were steps. The watch was passing. He could hear voices, a scurrilous jest. Yet they did not guess his presence in the gloom, and the clangor of their boots on the paving was gone with a closing door, and their laughter over the good story. In a moment he was after them in the great hall, turning away into the passage to the postern-gate.

The key creaked in the gate, and they were out in the mist, the gate closed and locked behind. The glare of the moonshine over the terrace and the water troubled Douglas. Any one who listened could pick them out with a musket. But he laughed since he had the keeper's keys, which held Loch Leven locked. But no time could be lost. They must go down to the bank to the skiff, which he saw was exactly where he had left it. A ladder at this point led to the landing. And while he would have helped her, the queen climbed down as easily as if she were a girl. She knew full well to her capture

The Loyalty of William Douglas

meant a captivity more odious than before, while to him, death.

When he pushed the boat the pebbles rattled enough to have aroused the castle. He gave the queen his hand, but she leaped in without aid. As the boat glided into the open loch the moon was hid by a scurrying cloud, and loch and castle held fast in mist and night. Douglas settled to the oars. Then at last the queen's voice came to him softly, —

"The sweet air! The freedom!"

"I would wish the oars were muffled."

As if to prove how noisy they were, a challenge rang out from Loch Leven. Lights passed against the windows. The alarm clanged.

"They have heard, or Master Ferguson has loosed his bonds!" said he. "But — ah, they 're locked in!"

Every key to every outer gate at Loch Leven was on that key-ring which had fascinated him. Dear key-ring was it indeed, which not only had given the means of escape, but which now could hold the pursuit. They would be forced to batter down a door before they could be after them. No wonder that it had been his desire so long; nor strange that he held it up before the queen's eyes gleefully, and then flung it far out into the lake, where it splashed, and where doubtless it lies to this day, rusted in the service of loyalty. What cared he now for the firing of the gun of Loch Leven, or the spent balls splashing over their bow? They could not see them in the welcome gloom, nor could they be out under an hour. The gates of that fortress were as well made as any in all Scotland.

Pulling on, Douglas found all at once his arm hurting much; for in some way, — likely in the struggle with the keeper, — it had been wrenched. Every stroke made it twinge. Finally he began to have a certain joy in resisting the pain, which was the pleasure of endurance. The firing continued; but they could only conjecture the position of the boat in that welcome gloom, and they began to find they were wasting powder. Douglas could imagine his aunt, her gown hastily thrown on, spending her rage. She had trusted him, and he had been untrustworthy, but for the queen.

"To the Edinboro' road? Do you know the landing there?"

"Well, your Grace."

"And the sign of the Deerhound?"

"A half-mile in."

"A good Scot mile, master. Our friends are there. I had the word in the laundress's linen."

By this time hard pulling had brought them close in shore, where he trusted to the sedges to shadow them. He thought to follow the shore to a spot near the Edinboro' road. The obscuring cloud was passing. Bushes brushed the skiff's sides. He thought he knew the waters, but found the boat scraping; it grounded. When, springing over and pushing out again, he took the oars, the moon reached out, casting a sheen over the waves, that danced in a little wind. Loch Leven showed out darkly across water, where was not a boat. The only danger was from the noise of the guns having attracted a passing troop of the regent. Equally would it warn the queen's friends that something was happening in the castle.

Douglas thought he should have to skirt the lake under the bushes. It would have been the height of folly to have ventured into that open space, to invite the marksmen of Loch Leven, or to excite the interest of those in the village, or chance passers on the highways.

He had been pulling the skiff without a word with his companion, only noting in the moonshine the outlines of her figure, her disordered hair, from which the cloak had fallen.

" Douglas ? "

" Your Grace ? "

" How have you dared this ? "

" You are queen."

" But, master, there is a king, my son ? "

" Your Grace, why should I side with this lord, or that, or with Lord James Stuart, when you are Mary Stuart, the queen in need ? "

" You were taught, Douglas, I was a criminal who have forfeited my right."

" I saw your Grace in distress."

" I never once suspected you would go to this extreme. I thought you only a page of the Douglases, I confess, master, and ask pardon."

" Your Grace, it does not become you to say such things to me. I have only done as others."

" But they never have. Your cousin tried, but failed."

" I may."

" We will not consider failure yet. But lest I never may have chance again, master, I wish to explain to you these charges. I cannot think you would believe them entirely. To you, Douglas, I would speak, although it is not the queen's part to explain."

For a moment she paused, while the bushes bent under the wind, the oars dipped, a wild-fowl called from the marsh.

" A young girl, my Douglas, came from the French court, where pleasure is almost duty, to austere Scotland, where of late some have held it sin. Many aspired to this princess's favor and love. If I — this girl queen — was thoughtless, I at first intended no evil. When I found my mistake, I hated those I had tricked with fancies. Darnley, whom I thought a hero, after all was imbecile; Rizzio but a sentimentalist, and Castelar — ? "

" And Bothwell ? " asked he in his interest, forgetting he had no right to ask.

" I fear him."

But she added : —

" I fear no man ! I am queen ! I will have blood for blood, eye for eye ! "

He had known this mood in the castle, when she would not see the keeper.

The Loyalty of William Douglas

"Those who have helped me," she went on, more gently, "shall have reward. I will have my own again. Yet — oh, Douglas, I am the unhappiest lady ever was born. So many who have served me have suffered bitterly."

"The queen shall have her own again!"

"She shall, for she will. And I am free, and in this bonnie land thousands are ready to die for us. Life is sweet as this brave air. Men still love me, and I may have some wit left."

The queen talked thus to William Douglas, because of her excitement more than from any intention to make of him a confidant.

He reached a place where he thought a landing prudent.

Taking his hand, she stepped to shore, where, pushing a way through the thick bushes, they came out on the expanse of the moor, reaching then up to the enclosure of the Deerhound.

The queen trudged on with her bundle,

The Loyalty of William Douglas

light-heartedly to appearance as a servant
lass who may be out with her lad for the
harvest dance.

"I see you take the way across the
moor because we there are less likely to
meet any one."

"Yes, I have no weapon, your Grace."

"Your knife —" she began.

"I left it," said he, "hum, hum, in
Jock, the guard."

He spoke thoughtlessly, and, as has been
the case with us all a thousand times,
would have given anything to have had the
words unsaid; for his companion lost her
gayety with the word. Her voice had a sob.

"My friend, don't bring to me the past
and its dead."

He felt the lout, and tried to murmur
some poor apologetic explanation, until she
interrupted with laughter, —

"No, you cannot make me saddish.
Across the moor we go, master."

And she led the way, humming a little
French air.

The Loyalty of William Douglas

" That's a gay song, Master Douglas, out of keeping with Scotch austerity."

" The Deil 's sometimes behind their gravity, your Grace," said he, trying to affect a lightish manner.

" Yes, horns and all. I 've seen him behind one of these dissenting ministers, again and again. Even John Knox acknowledged ' there 's not so much harm in a bonnie time as in a bad heart, but,' he added, ' your dancing will blacken your heart.' Eh, Douglas, mayhap he was right. How silent you are."

" I was wishing for a sword."

" How strange it is that you who have been brave should tremble. Come, my master, a little farther, and we shall be at the Deerhound."

He did not answer, for he had fancied he saw shadows like those of men : fearful lest some one might spring out of the bushes, and maddened to think how powerless he should be against some passer who certainly would be armed to the teeth.

The Loyalty of William Douglas

He, who in Queen Mary's time, carried life in an open way, was likely to have his right to it challenged at any moment by highwaymen, or his clan's enemy. The queen, to give him heart, again laughed.

"Have you not done that which the others failed in? Are we not almost with friends?"

"Ay, but who knows who their bell and cannon may not have stirred up? And — you know, your Grace, a bare hand has small favor with bare steel."

"It's a Scot's hand, Master Douglas! A Scot brain. We'll have no more French tunes this night. I know a better of your own people."

I fancy you who read may know that ancient song of the Douglas', — a catching tune that renders a Douglas proud of his own. Through it all runs the clash of steel, and the cry that rendered the race warm for the fray. Now it came in a low tone from a lady's lips, and it gave this Douglas heart. He had been shuddering at what he had done, but now again, with her voice, he cared not at all whom he should face. So curiously is bravery a matter of how the brain — or is it how the heart? — works. On that lonely moor, it was as if they two, queen and subject, had the world to themselves. The moon-shine makes the earth so different a place. A man makes love under the moon, to hate her under the sun.

A stone wall marked the enclosure of the Deerhound, and revealed the hazard.

" You can trust those you expect to be at the Deerhound? "

" As much as you. Go to the rear door. Knock thrice. To him asking your errand, say, ' Does the day please? ' "

" Yet something may have gone against us."

" The fortune of war," assented the queen.

" And do you, your Grace, remain here in the shadow of the wall until I may find how our fortune may be at the inn."

The Loyalty of William Douglas

" Wait, master ! "

She took from her bosom a little gold
crucifix.

" I must pray, Master Douglas. For
sinners was Christ, the priests tell us. I
would pray to him, for he is greater than
the Virgin, although likely she understands
us women."

He had bowed his head, if he had been
taught her faith was idolatrous.

" Father," said the queen, holding the
image high, " I pray Thee remember us.
Remember James, my son. Remember
William Douglas, my knight. O God
of Scotland, and of Mary Stuart, do Thou
hear the prayer of us who without Thee
are but babes in a wood."

What matters a man's faith so much as
his honesty ? A long time yet has the
world to learn that theology is naught
more than a trickery of phrases. Her
eyes were on him. Her belief in the
power of Him the little image symbolized
to help her for all her faults, impressed

him with a sort of ardor of entreaty to Him. He had been man; had suffered, been perplexed. He could understand all, even the murder of Jock, the guard. The words of the ministers of the New Church rang in William Douglas's memory; "O God, we are poor sinners indeed!"

"I believe you are one of the dissenters, master? They'd make light of our ancestors' faith. Are we, poor, conceited fools, so much wiser?"

She pressed the crucifix to her lips, and thrust it again into her bosom. She held out her hand, which he pressed to his lips, and turned to scale the wall without another glance back, yet hating to leave her so, fearful of all that might happen.

Dropping down on the farther side of the wall, he found himself in the stable yard of the Deerhound. No one appeared to be stirring, although lights were in the upper windows. About the corner of the house a train of light fell across the highway beyond, as if the front doors were wide.

The Loyalty of William Douglas

Finding the rear door without difficulty, he knocked once, twice, thrice. When there was no answer, although he fancied he heard voices, he again raised the knocker, which fell into its metal place with a far-reaching resonance. Again he lifted it, and again. Five minutes passed, when there was rustling, and then a stumbling inside. Somebody fumbled with bolts, and opened the door, keeping the chain on. A withered, wrinkled face looked out.

" What want you ? " questioned a husky voice.

"Good dame, does the day please ? " — albeit a night of the full moon.

The candle near dropped from her palsied hand.

" Wait," she said, like one of the Fates.

The door closed. So long a time passed that Douglas was about to turn back, or to try the other door. Should he be greeted by the Earl of Moray's followers ? He could hear his heart, he fancied. And what might be happening

behind the stone wall? Was she in
peril from he knew not whom? How
easily all his effort up to this might
be made naught! Nor were Lord Moray's
men alone to be feared. There were
hundreds of others during that unsettled
period who might be at the Deerhound,
inimical to the cause. You may believe
it was almost in fright he heard again a
rattling of the bolts.

This time the chain was loosed, when
the door opened, showing the dame, and
two others with travel-stained boots, but
so closely muffled that he could not make
them out, nor their style of dress. One
stepped up to him when he saw the eyes
peering from the cloak.

" Your question ? "

" I pray you, master, does the day
please ? "

The other thrust back his covering.

" Will ? Will Douglas! We heard the
cannon Loch Leven. And now you are
here with that question ? "

The Loyalty of William Douglas

Muffled as the speaker was, William Douglas could not be mistaken in the voice.

"Ah, cousin," said he, "we are of the same political complexion. I, as you, serve the queen, not Moray."

The other now was holding a lantern high, peering into his face.

"Blood on your cuff?"

The presence of one's relatives may lead to the assumption of any bravado one may own. Before our kin, most of all, we like to show best our prowess, our cleverness, our bravery, our all. So was it with William Douglas.

"I killed a fellow who stood in my way."

"And you are from the queen?"

"I came with the queen."

"Eh, boy! What's turned your sense?"

"Cousin," said he to George Douglas, "get me ladder with which to scale the wall, and you will understand I am no liar. Hurry, fools! The ladder, I tell you."

"You 're in your cups, Will Douglas."

"I have done that you failed in," he boasted.

"Your Grace," he cried.

"Master Douglas?"

"The queen's voice," said he.

George Douglas's incredulity vanished, and he was over the wall, where they found him kneeling before the Lady o' the Scots.

"Kneel not to me who owe much — yes, almost all — for freedom is all! — to the Douglases."

"We were your gaolers."

"Who have freed the prisoner."

"Not I, but my cousin."

"But, Douglas, you tried, if the other succeeded. Come, your hand, over the wall."

He did this gallantly with all his grace. But William Douglas had heard the queen's words. He had succeeded where his cousin failed. The cannon of Loch

The Loyalty of William Douglas

Leven had excited the inn, keeping the watchers for the queen awake. How many others, unfriendly to the restoration, might have been aroused, the queen's gentlemen then could only conjecture. If William Douglas's thought to leave the castle without the keys to unlock its doors had delayed the chase, yet now it were imprudent to tarry at the Deerhound.

Nor was it half an hour before the company was in the saddle, shouting under its breath, —

" God, and the queen ! "

With the steady swing of cantering horses, — the lighting of the sky in the east, the stirring of men and women along the way for their morning tasks, — they saw the tower of a queen's fortress.

But in the heart of William Douglas was no gladness ; and he wondered, for had he not succeeded ?

Yet the Fate that makes hearts said, " There shall be no success without a regret."

The Loyalty of William Douglas

II

And he who was the envy of the court that rallied quickly under the queen's banner, knew this, although men envied and the queen favored and knighted him, as the Douglas whose lealty atoned in degree for his relatives.

Queen o' the Scots was she again, the color in her cheeks, gracious to all, — to win back that she had lost.

But this Stuart princess had small time to think of minor matters, when her realm was disjointed and all her wit needful.

And William Douglas saw her rarely, and then, in the court formality. And again he was vexed, and only grew happier when in the fight ; and there were many fights in those days when Scotland was divided against itself, and some were for the queen and others for the regent.

And Sir William, as he was then because of the service he had done, found further distinction which was not to his heart. Yet a man cannot live with memories, although he may wish to die because of them.

And since he would forget, he tried to make love as well as to fight. In the little court was a Mistress Agnes Frazer — who did not disdain him; and the queen, hearing of this, sent for him.

"Ah, Douglas," said she, smiling prettily, as she could, "I have heard of you and my maid Agnes."

But Douglas was silent.

"Are you embarrassed, Douglas?" said she then, "that I should question?"

"Yes, your Grace," said he, sturdily.

"And why?"

"Because, your Grace, I have but tried to make love to Mistress Agnes, that I might forget."

"And why?" asked she, for they say she never was displeased at seeing the light that then was in his eyes.

"Your Grace," said he, "I must forget

The Loyalty of William Douglas

I'm unhappy, because no longer can I stand between you and danger."

Then she twitted him on practising a courtier's speeches, but noting him, she saw that same look, causing her to turn away. Yet she was not displeased.

But after this she avoided him, so that he, thinking he had displeased her, was the more downcast, and wondered at himself, why he should be so.

But he found that Mistress Frazer could not lighten the heart ; nay, even the battle-field failed.

Then again, William Douglas took the chances others held foolishly desperate, yet, as is the way when men wish him, Death did not seek him. Death, seeking us all, seldom comes when he is called, for he too seems to be ruled by mockery.

But there came a time when Death was piqued at William Douglas, always daring him. For after many days — when the loyal cause seemed again hopeless — William Douglas was sore wounded in the

thigh, and was borne away among others
to the castle where the queen chanced to
be lodged.

And one of her ladies came to the queen,
telling her among the wounded in the battle was Sir William Douglas.

And the queen remembered, and went
into the room where he lay, breathing
hard.

Being told he must die, she kneeled
down by him, and said softly, with tears
in her eyes, that she was losing all her leal
subjects, who were more than the crown
of Scotland, when Douglas opened his eyes
on her.

He appeared comelily boyish, as if he
were still in his promise; yet the queen
knew he had done her a strong man's
service.

"Live, Douglas, for me, your queen.
Happiness shall be yours. You shall
marry the prettiest lady of my suite, and
shall have all the land of a Scot county."

But he sighed, as with his hurt.

The Loyalty of William Douglas

" Your Grace, you 're fairer than all the ladies of your suite, and the memory of that night with you is more than all the lands of a Scot county."

And those who were there, saw the queen blush, and say very softly, " No loyalty is like your loyalty," and bending forward she pressed her lips to his and said again, " Yes, no loyalty is like yours," and rising, went away.

But when she heard that against all the predictions of the surgeons he had recovered, she was piqued, and held his loyalty not so great. And Douglas was even sorry that he had not died then, for he had wished to die. Nor did the queen remember that she had promised him all the lands of a Scot county; nor did he remind her, nor see her often.

But, poor queen, the Scot counties passed away from her, and she was a prisoner at the hands of Queen Elizabeth, against all the rules of hospitality.

Then she would mutter, they say,

The Loyalty of William Douglas

" There is no loyalty like that of William Douglas."

And William Douglas came to her by permission of Lord Shrewsbury, and was added to her suite.

But Queen Elizabeth, having heard of the episode at Loch Leven, ordered that he be dismissed.

But he swore that he would free her, as many another Scot gentleman did for that matter, and English and French lords, and the King of Poland.

Now, one day in her prison, Mistress Jane Kennedy, the queen's lady, told her that William Douglas had been killed in the last attempt to reach her and free her; which was fortunate, as, if captured, he certainly would have been executed with the English and Scot gentlemen who were in that plot. But the Queen of Scots would not believe that he was dead, and up to the last expected to see him again, — a proof, say the historians, that she was a bit maddened by that long imprisonment, when she became faded and hopeless, with only memory left of all her possessions and all her lovers.

But whether it were a mad or wise saying, it was ever a favorite one of hers, that " no loyalty was like that of William Douglas," and that he again would prove it. And she was a princess who attracted men's loyalty to madder extremes than any, whether by her majesty or her wantonness, her biographers disagree.

When Position Fails

When Position Fails

IN 1776 our representatives declared in the enthusiasm of the moment the paradox " All men are born free and equal." 'T was a neat enough statement for paper, but some in America believed it not. Was there an equal for General Washington? Did we not cringe a bit to rank when a French marquis — albeit a tall, red-haired boy — came among us? A title caught even then many a good appointment, and I doubt much sometimes if Alexander of New Jersey would have been so much esteemed if he had not had claim to the Scottish earldom of Stirling. I am sure many inefficient foreign adventurers had service with us because they had titles. Two of these gentlemen proved conclusively that they had great natural abilities : one, of course, Monsieur de la Fayette, who, a boy of twenty, came so cleverly out of the affair of Barren Hill, and the other, Casimir Pulaski, the Pole, whom I saw fall with a wound in the thigh during the charge on Savannah.   Taken on the brig "Wasp," he died as she was putting to sea, esteemed a good friend, a gallant captain.

It was only the night before that he told me the truth of that affair at Warsaw which led to his service in America.   He was not, the Count Pulaski assured me, himself a partner in this matter, although he was indeed a member of that Confederation of Bar, sworn to fight for Polish freedom to the very end.   But circumstantial evidence led to his banishment, as it had to that of so many others.   Despairing of Poland, and eager for a career, he came to America.

Yet although my friend was not himself in this affair, the story he told of it appears to me new.   The picture of the king and his assassin walking side by side, reasoning together of the rainy night in the wood of Bilany has had more than passing effect. The story proves that our revolt against a king was not the first. Ah, history is full of these instances, King John, Charles Stuart, Stanislaus of Poland, Louis XVI., George III. by proxy in America, and many another.

Now this is the account of the affair as I remember it — of the Street of the Capuchins, Warsaw.

The king had been to his summer palace that day of September 3d, 1771, and his coach was returning along the Street of the Capuchins. Now it was nine o'clock of a rainy night as the leader of the king's guard of some seventeen dragoons was astounded by a man leaping before his horse with the loud command, " Halt." The lieutenant struggled to bring his sabre down on the fellow's head. His horse careened, stopping indeed the whole company and the coach, whence the king's head suddenly projected.

At the moment a shot, from a window of a supposedly deserted house, grazed the king's face, instantly killing the servant who was with him in the coach.

" The king is assassinated," the cry was raised from guards and passers. " His Majesty is dead ! "

Stanislaus, who ever was considerate of his inferiors, shouted at this, —

" It is Felix, the *heyduc*, who is shot. Quick, catch the assassin ! "

Suddenly down the street came the sounds of horses, and cries, —

" Down with Stanislaus, the creature of the Russians ! "

At the same instant men rushed out of the house whence the shot into the coach had come, swearing, shouting, and firing. One of the king's guards cried, —

" A plot ! An ambush ! There are a thousand ! "

Instantly the panic became general.

When Position Fails

The lieutenant of the Guards, who had succeeded in running through the fellow at his bridle rein, now found himself confronted by the horsemen. Turning, he led the flight, and the king was left almost alone in his coach, hugging the dead body of his poor servant, and oblivious to everything else. The horses on the coach, rearing and plunging, required all the attention of the postilions, who themselves were frightened out of whatever wit they may have had.

By this time the leader of the attacking horsemen was dismounted by the coach door.

"Out, Stanislaus!" he cried, "you are to come with me."

The king, perceiving who this was, cried out to him, —

"Kolinski, traitor, I am your king."

For an instant Kolinski hesitated. The sight of the king, placed as he was, with the dead servant in his arms, and yet, still the king, with that dignity Stanislaus always possessed — that scene shown dimly by the lantern of the coach, shook for a moment the conspirator's resolution.

But the others were behind him, desperate, and knowing that if the issue of the adventure were not successful death was certain.

" Pull him out ! "

Then Stanislaus looked up from the dead *heyduc* in his lap, the dark, handsome man he always was, now with no fear, but with a mastering anger at the indignity.

" You shall hang for this ! "

Ah, they knew that danger too well. They could not hesitate, if pity for a moment had weakened their purpose.

Roughly they dragged the king from the coach, he struggling and crying and clinging to the dead, and the sides of the coach.

I can imagine nothing more horrible than that scene, — the king now outside in the mud, the dead body of the ser-

vant dangling from the coach step, the
postilions struggling with their horses,
the conspirators, some on foot and some
mounted, surrounding the king, one bringing the flat of a sabre against his head, and
the crowd of townspeople who suddenly
had gathered.

And then a cry went up, —

" The Guards are returning ! "

Kolinski was on his horse now, and he
caught the king, who between the struggle,
and horror at his dead servant, was in a half
dazed state. Another seized Stanislaus's
other shoulder.

" The Guards ! " rang out the cry again,
" The Guards ! "

Kolinski lashed his horse, dragging the
near lifeless king. On they tore, Kolinski
again and again having to slacken his
horse's speed, lest the king should be
killed. So much more slowly was the
progress made by those who were dragging the king that the others, now seized
with panic, ran as they could; and when

the ditches beyond the city were reached, only seven remained. Here Kolinski paused, uncertain about the path in the darkness, densened by the rain. They were outside the city with their captive, but whither should they take him? Kolinski cursed. The king braced himself without a word against the dripping horse. Stanislaus had lost a shoe. His foot was torn and bleeding. Never was man or king in sorrier plight.

"Do you remember, sire, that you danced at the palace last night?" Kolinski asked with bitter mockery.

"Ah, fallen king!" said Stanislaus, "I remember, and can foresee, wretch, how high you will hang."

"Hang!" muttered Kolinski at this. "Ah, I may."

In the mean time one of the others called back, —

"This is the way."

Kolinski then spurred up his horse, again dragging the king. But the way was uneven. He stopped to dismount, releasing Stanislaus for an instant.

"Yes, we shall have to walk," said one of the others. "But where are we?"

"In the wood of Bilany," Stanislaus himself answered.

"Yes, but where?" asked Kolinski, peering into the gloom. The rain trickled from the leaves, and then came stealthy movements.

"The Russians!" whispered one. "The Russians!"

"A patrol?" questioned another. "Quick! Save yourselves!" Panic seized them, as it had the others. They disappeared among the trees, into the darkness.

Then the king laughed, a jarring, mocking laugh.

"Kolinski, my captors have fled. We are alone — you and I. Come, let me go. We are man to man."

"Man to man, Pole against Russian.

When Position Fails

I have sworn, Stanislaus, to take you. I'll not give you up."

"But can I not call out to the Russians?"

"Bah! Cry out! Do you fancy they would believe you were the king, or that they could hear? I do not believe they were Russians, but only the panic fears of my friends."

"And you have no fear, Kolinski?"

"Fear? Yes, I have enough of it. But I am little less likely to die — and I have no wish to die — if I carry this out."

And here the king interrupted by shouting at the top of his voice.

"How useless!" said Kolinski, trying to put his hand over his mouth. "Do you not see that you are as likely to be heard by my friends, who will hasten to help me, as by a Russian patrol?"

The king, who was much exhausted, as one may believe, had thrust Kolinski's hand aside. Now he said, —

" Ay, true."

" But where are we?" asked Kolinski.

" I know not save in the wood of Bilany."

" We must walk and find out. We cannot go over these ruts with the horse."

" We must walk," said the king. " It avails neither of us to stand as we are in the rain."

And leaving the horse, they walked on through the dripping wood, not knowing the direction, although Kolinski was careful to take that which he thought led away from Warsaw. And as this odd pair stumbled on, the king sore and sad and weak, so that Kolinski, he knew, would have no difficulty in controlling him alone, the king said, —

" Villain, you shot my servant, Felix."

" I would to heaven it had been your Majesty."

" And in what have I wronged you, Kolinski?"

When Position Fails

"As you have every Pole, by ruling Poland for her enemy's sake."

"Yes, granted, man, that may be the fact. But how do you know that I may not think it for the better?"

"And why?"

"Because you Poles cannot rule yourselves, nor would you let me."

"No, we have stolen your Majesty that you may not rule."

"And how did you get into Warsaw without arrest?" said the king; when the other answered, —

"Your Majesty need not suspect your police in this matter. We entered disguised as peasants, and some of us hid in hay-carts."

Now in this strange conversation without any farther appeal by the king to his companion's pity, Kolinski yet in some way was influenced. They both were equally lost in the wood of Bilany, captive and captor, and, now that Kolinski reflected about the matter, he saw that it

was equally necessary for both to find
some way out. Yet he must not let the
king escape him. His freedom, nay, his life
probably depended on him keeping the king.

After stumbling along, the rain now
having stopped, the pair noticed a light
through the trees.

" The Convent of Brelany ! " said the
king.

With a cry of dismay Kolinski recognized the building, which declared that for
all their walking they had proceeded in a
circle, the convent not being a league from
Warsaw.

" Shall we ask aid of the nuns ? " the
king asked.

For answer the other clutched his arm.

" Not on your life, fool ! " he cried.

As he spoke, the great gate was suddenly
thrown back, casting a bar of light over a
sodden road, and the dripping oaks beyond. Out of the gate came slowly an
old monk, stumbling along. Kolinski
clutched the king's arm the tighter, know-

ing that he was lost should the monk dis-
cover them. But the door closed, the
monk passed down the road. The place
was still, when suddenly the notes of the
organ in the convent chapel broke in on
the silence. The king crossed himself,
muttering a prayer.

"For my *heyduc*, Felix, whom you
killed, man."

"Come," said Kolinski, roughly. "We
cannot wait here."

The king followed, and again Kolinski
wondered why the king had not tried to
communicate with the monk.

"Why did you not speak? Why do
you come with me?" he asked curiously,
after a moment. "Why, man, do you
not struggle with me?"

"Because, Kolinski, I would win you."

The count paused at that. Again they
were in the forest. Again he was not
certain of their path; but it was not or
this uncertainty he was thinking now, but
of the king.

"Why did you not cry out to the monk?"

"You would have been caught."

"Of course, but so much the better for you."

"No," answered the king, "so much the worse, Kolinski."

"And why, I have asked?"

"Count, has not to-night proven how much the King of Poland needs friends, — strong, daring men?"

"And you are trying to gain me?"

"I am trying to gain you."

Count Kolinski was ever most suspicious; now he saw the king's cunning, he thought, in endeavoring to gain him.

And suddenly he asked himself why would it not be better for him to side with the king? The issue of the adventure was uncertain. He was alone with the captive, who, of course, was disabled with the wound in his foot and the rough usage. He, Kolinski, easily could let the king escape. It would be easy to persuade his fellow conspirators that he had been forced to abandon the captives, as all the others indeed had. By aiding the king he might purchase for himself immunity. The thought was tempting, possibly more so because of a certain dignity with which Stanislaus had borne himself since the first of the adventure. Kolinski felt himself, you may see, grasping a horn of the dilemma he had not thought possible. And as he thought of his position he remembered the strong oath he had taken to carry out his object.

"Come!" he began.

"But—" Stanislaus began.

"I have sworn, sire!" began Kolinski, almost humbly, for he understood well the significance in the " but."

Stanislaus threw himself on the ground wearily.

"Ah!" said the other, with sudden pity, "I had forgot your wound."

"Yes, Count Kolinski, you have forgot much."

" And what, sire ? "

" That he who takes an oath against his king takes no binding one."

" Sire, it is Poland's interest I have sworn to protect.   And yet — "

" And yet, Kolinski ? "

" This night I have grown to think differently of you.   I have come to respect you as a man."

" A king is but more — or less — than a man."

" The King of Poland I held less up to this night."

" And have you changed ? "

" If I should free you I should be taken — executed."

" Count," said the king at this, for Stanislaus had a shrewd wit in times of need, " if I be more than a man, a king, my oath should be good, and I swear to you that you shall meet no harm. Should my guards come on us now I would direct them to the road contrary to that you take."

When Position Fails

" If I could believe you ! "

" And why should you not ? "

" You have suffered so much from me."

" You can believe me if you will reflect."

" And why ? " asked Kolinski, again wondering.

" Because I want your brain, your daring. Should I persuade you I should have you as my servant."

" True," Kolinski reflected. Some creatures stirred in the forest. A little wind waved the trees, and swept their faces. The phases of the matter presented themselves. Which was the better, the safer ? To serve the king ? Certain he would be a fool not to, should the king succeed or fail. The scene in the Street of the Capuchins occurred to him again, — the king with the dead servant in his arms, lit by the fitful glare of the lantern of the coach. The wandering in the forest had changed his idea of Stanislaus.

When Position Fails

" You are the king, sire. Forgive me — if you may."

Ah, could he after that night's adventure! For the moment he hesitated again. Suddenly Stanislaus extended his hand to him.

" Thank you, Count Kolinski."

" But I have not said."

" I know your thoughts. It is your interest to serve me, they tell you, count."

" I have thought that, sire."

And then with the quickness with which daring men arrive at decisions, he cried :

" I will serve you. They — my comrades — have run, leaving it all for me to do. My interest is with you, sire."

" If I had not thought you would arrive at this conclusion I should have cried out to the monk," Stanislaus answered ; " for do you not see how truly your interest is with me ? It is doubtful should I resist if you could get me to your friends. On the other hand we both are lost in the forest. We need each other."

283

When Position Fails

" I have considered that, sire."

At this they were groping their way again, the king saying that they must be near the mill of Mariement. They had come on a path which he was certain was one he remembered when hunting in that part of the wood.

By this time the clouds lifting somewhat, they were able to see that the conjecture might prove true, and presently they heard the brook tumbling over its stony bed below the raceway of the mill.

At the door of the low darkened building Kolinski knocked, once, twice, thrice and again. When there was no response he grew impatient.

" Where do you suppose the miller of Mariement may be ? " he asked.

" Inside, thinking we may be robbers," said the king.

At this Kolinski picked up a stone and sent it crashing through the window, while he shouted,—

" Open to the king."

Then there came a light, and an old man's fretful tone,—

" What want you ? "

" The king is here at your door, rascal; open ! "

The miller was not persuaded even then. But at last between his fear and curiosity he opened his door. And even then he had difficulty in recognizing Stanislaus in the miserable figure the king made after his sorry experience.

" Pardon, sire," he cried, falling on his knees. " Pardon."

" Up, man; I do not wonder. The Count Kolinski and I were set on by assassins in the forest."

" Assassins ! " cried the miller of Mariement.

" Yes, assassins," Stanislaus answered, while he pushed into the bare little room where the miller's wife and son stood staring their astonishment.

Kolinski now began to tremble for himself. Would Stanislaus keep his word with him now? The king's manner had changed. He was writing to General Coccei of the Guards in Warsaw:

"By a kind of miracle, I am saved from the assassins. I am here at a little mill of Mariement. I am wounded, but not badly."

He called to the miller, who was now eager enough to gain the royal favor, to carry the letter to Warsaw.

While they waited, Kolinski again hesitated, but being a brave man, he saw that regrets availed him nothing. Possibly Stanislaus was equally suspicious of him. At any rate they both showed their relief in their faces when General Coccei, who had believed the king to be dead, arrived at the mill door in his carriage.

But then again Kolinski trembled.

"He is one of the conspiracy, sire. I have proof positive," the General of the Guards declared.

"Proof positive!" Stanislaus answered

smiling. "I have proof positive that Count Kolinski has saved my life."

Kolinski had listened to every word.

"Sire," said he at last, "am I indeed pardoned?"

"Hush," said Stanislaus, "we are friends. Our fortune lies together. Your friends will accuse you of siding with me. Ah, you have."

"You have the proof, your Excellency," Kolinski said, turning to the commandant of the Guards. He had courage. The adventure of the wood had changed his politics, nay, his opinions. Stanislaus appeared to him as he was, a likable gentleman, misplaced as King of Poland.

In the event Stanislaus kept his word given in his desperation. He had seen during that strange walk they had taken together, how clever a man Kolinski was. He alone received pardon, he alone of all the conspirators escaped the fiat of the Polish law.

Two of the conspirators, Strawenski

and Lowenski, accused him very bitterly
of their betrayal.   They execrated him as
they ascended the scaffold.

But Count Kolinski answered the
charge boldly.   He said the other conspirators abandoned him.   He could not
keep the king without aid.   When he
had discovered that Stanislaus was inclined
to be clement he had accepted his cle-
mency, and the king had kept his word.
However erroneous Stanislaus's political
opinions and practices might have been, he
at least had not lied in this : was ever, as
far as he was able to be, the good friend of
those who supported him.   At least Count
Kolinski declared, that the " man " was
greater than the " opinion."

If these declarations were influenced by
fear, I am sure that Count Kolinski had
good, prudent reasons for his conduct.
At least I have a very vivid picture of the
strange scene between king and conspirator, of the rainy night in the wood.   I fear
I have not made the scene so clear as the

account Casimir Pulaski gave of the adventure that began with the abduction in the Street of the Capuchins.

On the last night of Casimir Pulaski's life, as I have said, he told me this. The morrow was to bring the fatal assault before Savannah. Possibly the whole scene is more vivid to me on account of that memory. For Count Pulaski, although we were very jealous of foreigners, was a most excellent captain, as his achievement in the Southern department showed.

That he served with us at all was entirely due to the adventure of which I have given a poor enough description, and in which, although it led to his banishment, he himself had no part. Although I have heard many stories to the contrary, I have no reason to doubt the strict truth of this statement, for in my own experience I ever found Casimir Pulaski a man of his word.

Angela

Angela

THE scandal-mongers of the wheel are confined mostly to those who cannot, or do not, wheel. Not so long ago women were likely to make mental faces at other women who rode, but so soon as they themselves were spinning along with a freedom they never had fancied, they straightway wondered at all these allegations. And how, indeed, does a brisk turn under the sky, and between the fields, drive away cobwebby notions! In the old days a canter might do it ; but a horse is a luxury, and, even if you can afford it, is ever getting out of condition, and to be fit must have a modicum of constant exercise. But now all go a-spinning, the horseman as well as the one-time long-distance walkers, the sinners and those who strive to regain this old world from the curse.

Angela

Among these latter, no one is better equipped for the ancient fight than the rector of St. Matthew-in-the-Park, the Rev. Lemuel Springer. With body and mind attuned to a fine healthfulness, at thirty, he believes strongly, and preaches and acts his belief; and in these days when clergymen sometimes forget that their duty is but to heal the heart's wounds, and to preach the reward of simple honesty and cleanly living, it is a delight to sit of a morning in a pew of St. Matthew-in-the Park and listen to the direct and human religion its athletic young rector expounds. I, myself, remember him when he was No. 3 on the 'Varsity crew, and a very great man. He still could pull that third oar as strongly, but the only sport his duties now permit him is wheeling, and if you go to the park of a morning you may see him going up and down hill, and doubtless meditating those words for the soul-cheer afforded by his bits of sermonizing, put always in English tersely strong.

Angela

And yet he has had his troubles, his experiences, his questionings, his sin, his falsity; and if you will follow my story, you will see how it all was due to the wheel that he once forgot himself.

Of a May day the Reverend Lemuel was coasting down the long hill into the straggling village of Roundbush, Westchester. It was his day of outing, and now at noon he was hungry after a twenty-mile exhilarating spin; and the world had put its care away, and his blood was tingling and his heart singing like the birds in the fields and the treetops through the windy blue spaces of that sunny spring-day sky. The old tavern at Roundbush bears on a creaking sign a distorted likeness of our first great President, and after long years of desuetude again has found usefulness through the revival of the road, and flaunts a noon placard: "Lunches for Bicyclers." Yet this afternoon the Reverend Lemuel thought that he had it quite to himself, as the fat landlord pushed his shirt-sleeves farther above his brawny elbows and said he guessed he could give his visitor " somethin' that was fit eatin'." And Lemuel — I will drop his title — thought the broiled chicken delicious, and sauntered into the parlor, dark after the sunshine, with its haircloth chairs and its colored prints of " Washington Crossing the Delaware," and " John Brown's Capture," and certain photographs of prim rural folk.

Now usually Lemuel was most observing, yet he had been in that room fully five minutes before he noticed a figure stretched out on a couch; at the dark side, to be sure, so indeed it may not have been so strange that he had not seen her at first. Her face sunk in a pillow, she seemed to be sobbing. Lemuel at once made for the door, when he heard a sweet and strangely plaintive voice : —

" I 'm such a fool ! Oh, I beg your pardon ! " she added, with such evident confusion that Lemuel turned about hastily to see the prettiest figure of a woman in a witching bicycle costume; and what she was like I'll leave you to fancy : just fancy, that is, the very nicest girl of your acquaintance, and you will see her as Lemuel saw her much more easily than from any description of mine.

"Oh!" she said hastily, rubbing her eyes.

"I beg your pardon," said Lemuel.

"It was my fault," she said, looking him over demurely. "I forgot this was a public room."

"I am sure it was mine," said Lemuel, hastily. It was all rather strange and sudden, and yet he decided at once that she was a well-bred young person.

"Oh, I am glad," she exclaimed.

"I don't see why," he blurted out in astonishment.

"Because you are Mr. Springer of St. Matthew-in-the-Park."

He bowed, remembering with a bit of conceit that a lot of people doubtless knew him whom he did n't know from Adam or Eve.

" I need a clergyman," she said.

Now at this astounding statement Lemuel stared his utter astonishment. Did she need his spiritual advice ? She looked a bit worldly.

" That is rather a surprising statement," she added.

" I don't know," he said, hopelessly.

" I mean," she said, " I want an escort to Greenwich, and with a clergyman there can be no question."

" I don't know," said Lemuel again.

" You must think me strange."

He looked at her for a moment, and made a very worldly reply, —

" I think you delightful."

" You will let me go with you, then ? "

" Why, of course, if you ask me," he said ; and why in the world did he say exactly that ?

" I do — and we must be started before him."

" Him ? — I don't understand."

" I will explain later; we must be
started now. We have no time."

" Oh, no time ? "

" Can you oblige me, Mr. Springer ? "
And with those eyes on him he could
and did, and having paid his reckoning he
was in the saddle, this graceful young person beside him, again and again looking
over her shoulder. She kept up a brisk
pace, neither saying a word, although you
may believe he was wondering at the impulse which had brought him to such
sudden complaisance. What if any of his
parishioners should see him as he was now,
tearing madly up and down hill with this
undeniably very pretty young woman, and
running madly from Him ? Who the deuce
was " Him ? " — only, of course, Lemuel
did n't say " who the deuce."

" Oh! oh! " she cried suddenly.

" Ah, what 's the matter ? " said he,
slowly.

" If he should appear, and attempt

to speak to me, you must knock him down."

"That would be rather unclerical, would n't it ? " said Lemuel.

" You must," said she.

" Oh, if I must," said he, looking at her, and knowing he certainly would.

The road forks half a mile further, with, at the point, a bit of wood and thicket. As you near the wood, you have the stretch of the road to the left, and now, as they came into that view, Lemuel's companion cried out, —

" Oh, I saw him ! "

" Who ? "

" No matter ; we must hide. I don't believe he could have seen me," she added quickly.

And dismounting, she dragged her wheel after her into the bushes.

" You stay there," she called. " If he asks if you have seen me, you must say you have n't." And she disappeared.

" That would be a lie, would n't it ? "

" I have no patience with a man who can't lie when it's necessary," came back the answer. And all was still, save for the rural noises of the sunny May day. But at last about a turn came a wheelman. He was young and well groomed. Seeing Lemuel, he paused.

" Have you passed a young lady, sir?"

" What sort of a young lady?" said Lemuel, avoiding the lie direct.

" Wheeling."

" A half dozen, I think," said Lemuel, truly, breathing a sigh of relief.

For our young gentleman was in his saddle, and tearing on.

Five minutes passed; but presently a face appeared in a leafy frame, — a laughing, tantalizing face, — when she followed, dragging the wheel.

" He did n't see me."

" Now what does this mean?" Lemuel asked rather angrily.

" Is your patience worn out?" said she, demurely.

" Yes, I think it is. What's your name ? "

" Angela."

" Angela what ? "

" I am not going to tell you."

" But you know mine."

" Everybody does," said she, with gentle flattery.

" Oh, I don't know. But what does it mean ? "

" Now, please don't be angry — please." And she added, —

" You 've been so good."

" Have I ? " said he.

" Yes; I don't know what I should have done if you had n't appeared just then. You make me able to say if any one should see me, ' Why, I am out with Mr. Springer, and he is a clergyman.' "

" Oh, dear ! " said Lemuel.

" Now don't bother, please ! We 'd better be on the road."

And she mounted.

" Come on ! " she cried.

And when he was by her side she began again,

"I'll explain as I ought. There was a girl, and she thought she loved a man."

"Yes, I have heard of girls like that."

"But she did n't really."

"Yes, I know."

"How do you ?"

"Hum — I have a parish."

"So you have. Well, to go on: when she hears that man is engaged to another girl, she tries to 'cut' the other girl out, — out of pique, not love for the man, you understand."

"No, I don't."

"Well, you are not so clever as I thought. But to return to this girl — "

"Angela ?"

"Yes, she was Angela, if you will. Angela encourages the man — "

"The man who just passed ?"

"Tom, we 'll call him."

"Yes, Angela encourages Tom; and Tom succumbs — "

"Do you think so?" she said, looking at him mischievously. "Yes, he did: I must be frank with you, a clergyman. And it goes on — in a country house in Westchester in May. But there's small chance in a house party, you know."

"Yes, I know," said he.

"Of course you know, because you are a young clergyman of a modish church. Now — to go on with the story — Angela agrees to meet Tom on the wheel. She wheels for a long time before the appointed hour, and, getting tired, stops, as you know; and, being tired, her conscience pricks her."

"I know of such cases," said Lemuel, laconically.

"And she thought of the other girl, and remembered how wicked she has been, because she has been encouraging Tom just for fun."

"She should have felt wicked," said Lemuel, severely.

"Just then she sees a very prominent young clergyman."

" Oh, no," said Lemuel, becomingly.

" Well, at once she snatches the chance. She will appear to Tom when he meets her to be out with the clergyman. If he speaks she will ignore him. Should he persist, the clergyman, who is the stronger, will knock him down."

" Will he ? "

" Yes, he promised."

" Did he ? "

" Yes, because Angela wished it."

" Well, perhaps. But when Tom appears why does Angela run into the bushes ? "

" Don't you think it was better to avoid the meeting ? "

" Possibly."

" And now," she said, dismounting and extending a hand, " good-by."

" You are going to leave me ? "

" I live over there."

" There are a lot of houses. Greenwich, is n't it ? "

" Yes, Greenwich ; but no matter which

house. You are going back to town. I am ever so much obliged to you. You have been ever so good."

"Angela," he said, "must it be good-by?"

"Yes."

"And you won't flirt any more?"

"I never do."

"But you have confessed to it — with Tom."

"I never will again. Now good-by, Mr. Springer."

And she was in her saddle, and smiling back at him, and vanishing over the slope, leaving him rubbing his eyes.

At first he thought he would follow, but then in Greenwich he likely would meet some one who knew him, and he could not afford to appear ridiculous, particularly after such an escapade.

Yet, as he wheeled, he regretted his resolution, and he envied Tom, and he could n't think of his sermon; and he really was on that ride simply to clarify his mind that he might make his next discourse a fitting one.

And back at his desk, it was the same, and his sermon was singularly poor that next Sabbath morning.

And he strove with himself, and tried to put her out of his mind, and to think of how scandalous it all would seem to any of his parishioners who should hear of it. Yet he yielded, so far as to find himself looking about furtively for Angela. He even, with some self-deception, wheeled several times over the same roads.

But when he understood how impulse was carrying him, he lashed himself mentally as a hermit of old did his flesh. And he wrote a mighty sermon, which quite astonished his congregation; and after he had delivered it he was compelled out of consistency to give up his one indulgence surviving from a great career as a college athlete.

And he plunged deeper into his work, and "God's poor" and suffering never had more attention in that parish.

Angela

But he could n't give up dinners and routs altogether, as a certain attendance on these functions is plainly a clergyman's duty. And at one of these he saw Angela, and was presented. And under her eyes he forgot himself, as, Heaven knows, clergymen are as the rest of us.

"Angela," he began, "I have been looking for you."

"Have you?" said she.

"And Tom?" he asked, fearfully.

"Oh, he 's married."

"To whom? I did n't catch your name. Was it Mrs. —?"

"No, it is n't. It was — the other girl."

"I hope you have followed my advice," he said, after a moment.

"Not to — I told you I never did."

"I wish — I really wish you would make me the exception," said the Reverend Lemuel.

And the parish gossips — save, to be sure, certain dowagers, and prim, acidulous

Angela

virgins — declare that Angela, the rector's lady, shows the rule of an outrageously lively young woman turning sedate if her fancy and faith may be caught and held: all of which, of course, is fitting the curtain-fall on a comedy.

The Mermaid and the Duffer

The Mermaid and the Duffer

I

IN the first place Jack met a mermaid.
Don't be astonished, for she was near
it; a very modern, strong-limbed girl, with
hair and eyes like those in Señor Cabanel's
famous Venus, who could swim like a fish,
and who could entice you into flirtation, as
the mermaid of the old story. For it indeed seems as if all the old mythological
tales may be proven in these later days,
when your entrancing girl can swim, and
sail, and golf, and wheel, and ride, and
shoot, and bring down a partridge as easily
as a skilfully shot glance may fetch a too
susceptible man tumbling to her feet.
Jack saw Miss Spencer that very first
evening at Pierre Van Brule's, and the
light lay golden over the wave crests, and

315

she with the others came out of the surf, and her laughter fell like music on his ears, tired with the dry monotonies of the civil courts.

"She's my sister-in-law, Priscilla Spencer," Pierre explained to his guest. "The surf is fine to-day."

"Yes, jolly," said Priscilla, over his shoulder. The maid had wrapped her in a bright-colored surtout, and she stood there with dripping yellow hair, and mocking, mischievous eyes. Two bronzed young fellows sauntered behind; he noted their swelling muscles, their glowing, ruddy cheeks, and tangled hair. "Tom Brinton and Phil Merrivale, you know," Van Brule went on.

"Yes," said Jack, slowly, watching the girl.

"And Priscilla, Mr. Merton," said Van Brule.

"Ah, I am glad to know you. We all hear so much of you, Mr. Merton," said she.

The Mermaid and the Duffer

"You are thinking of Sandford and Merton," said Merrivale, who was of our day at New Haven.

"No, I am thinking of John Merton, the corporation counsel," said Priscilla, giving him a cool, dripping hand.

"I declare, I don't believe I shall do else but think of you for the rest of my days — Pierre's sister-in-law," said Jack, not stupidly at all, and Pierre thought that Amy, the hostess, might have been wrong when she said she was fearful lest Merton prove too heavy for the rest of that crowd. A clever man like that is all right anywhere, Pierre mused sententiously, in which, as the context will show, he was quite in the wrong.

"We shall meet at dinner," said Priscilla, nodding back, and then ran up the path to the red-shingled house, which stands on the cliff over the stretching sea, where you can hear ever a murmur of tragedy, against the comedy of summer lives.

The Mermaid and the Duffer

Now that answer to Priscilla was the one easy remark that Merton made during all the eventful visit. It was not indeed a studied remark, but rather the expression of a premonition. His uneasiness began in the drawing-room before dinner.

The Van Brules ended the long summer day by dining at nine o'clock. The dinner-coated crowd, the damsels in fluffy things — that show simplicity at the cost of heavy checks from papas or guardians or husbands — seemed very conventional after that first scene by the sea. But it was all surprisingly delightful after the hot, struggling town Merton had left — so the splendor of Paris once burst on me from the bright days of the storm on the North Atlantic. Merton was like an American in a Parisian drawing-room, who can't understand the flow of phrases, — a play of sport around him, animating all, which lay quite beyond his immediate comprehension. They talked of boating and swimming, and wheeling and golfing and records, and events in the circle where all were intimates. He was an outsider; a savage suddenly admitted. He could have told them of a world they did not know, of affairs; but they only would listen with polite acquiescence, voting him a bore. He saw that at once. He felt vaguely chagrined. His self-esteem, pampered by so many successes, was piqued. The hostess tried to put him at his ease, but confided afterward to Van Brule that he quite tired her out. Finally the mermaid entered; no, not the mermaid, but a demure, laughing Priscilla. She was quite a different being. Tom Brinton was at once at her side. Merton's eyes followed the pair with vague envy of their apparent intimacy. The butler gravely threw back the doors.

"You will take Priscilla, Mr. Merton," said the hostess.

"You have me, you see," said Priscilla.

"I am delighted," stammered our successful attorney, suddenly feeling an increased awkwardness.

"Oh, I have heard so much of you," gushed Priscilla.

"Yes, you said it. I don't believe you a bit," he declared, with the desire to assert himself. Why should he be put in the background by these popinjays? He referred to Brinton and Merrivale as those vain birds.

"Oh, you are trying to steal my — lightning. That should have been thunder, should n't it?"

"It lies in your eyes," said he. "Never trouble about quotations."

"You are awfully clever, and sarcastic, I believe."

"No, I am not; I mean it." She easily saw that he did indeed.

"Now I will return your remark. You are like all men."

"Am I?"

"No, I did n't mean that; you have done a lot of things. What I meant is that you have the art of the compliment."

"You should separate sincerity from insincerity."

"I think I do," said she. She thought him sincere, and her feminine instinct never lied to her, although it did to men.

"But seriously —" she began.

"I am serious —"

"Do you wheel?"

"Is that serious?"

"No —" He paused. He knew she would hold him in contempt if he said he did n't. He hesitated, and was lost.

"Yes — of course. I meant I am not an expert."

"Tom!" she called across the table to Brinton, "Mr. Merton is going with us on that thirty-mile spin to-morrow."

"Am I?" said he, startled at having the magnitude of his lie so suddenly thrust back on him.

"Why — don't you want to go?" said she.

The Mermaid and the Duffer

"Yes, awfully; but — I am a bit of a duffer."

"Ah, we know better."

"Do come along, Merton. Van Brule has a stable filled with wheels and horses," said Tom Brinton, although he plainly did not relish the notion.

"Oh, yes, Jack," said the host. "I'll speak to Ferguson to-night."

"Ferguson is the groom," Priscilla explained. "You must come along."

"And he will have a wheel ready for you. You people are to start at eight, I am told," the host went on.

"Yes, we are early birds."

"Now, I don't believe I will," said Jack. "It's awfully good of you. But you see I'm a duffer, as I said — out of practice. You go to-morrow without me, and I will practise a bit and be in condition day after to-morrow. You know I've been so busy lately that —"

He went on while the others mildly expostulated. His lie had caught him, but he would be up early to-morrow, and learn before anybody was around. Every wretched fool could learn to ride a wheel, and he would take a couple of hours by himself. He breathed more freely, for he was insistent that he would n't go. But presently another question from Miss Priscilla staggered him.

" And you golf? "

He had been caught in his first lie, so he answered bravely enough this time:

" No, I don't."

" You miss a lot," and he saw he was falling rapidly in her esteem. The meantime the table were talking the golfing lingo.

" I am sure Mr. Merton does everything, Priscilla," laughed the hostess.

" But I don't golf," he repeated stubbornly, now rather wishing that he had said that he did.

" We will have some rides, anyway, Mr. Merton," continued the hostess.

" I shall expect them," said Merton. He did sit a horse rather awkwardly.

The Mermaid and the Duffer

"And some swims," said Priscilla, which spurred him on.

"If there is one thing I do better than another it is swimming," he said.

"Oh, I am so glad. You know I'd rather be in the surf than to eat."

"I saw that," said he, remembering the mermaid.

As they rose from the table Tom Brinton in some way edged to Priscilla's side, and presently had her to himself. Our great young attorney fell moody. What a detestable beast Brinton was! Why the dickens had he been slaving all his life, when these chaps had all the ease which he lacked; and they were but triflers. Ah, they knew the urbanities, which, after all, were worth while. And he — he tried to talk to several young women, conscious all the time of dismal failure. On the beach, under the moon, he could see Priscilla walking with Brinton. Confound Tom Brinton; you see reason suddenly had left this hitherto most reasonable man, — left him as a coquette may her victim.

"I believe I will turn in, Pierre, if you don't mind. I'm a bit tired."

"I know you have been in that horribly musty office, wearing yourself out," said the hostess.

"Oh, no," he said, "your delightful hospitality puts that out of the way." Just then he heard Priscilla : —

"Won't you change your mind about that expedition to-morrow?"

She stood on the lower step. Tom Brinton's cigarette glowed by her side.

"I think I'll remain firm by my resolve," he said laughingly.

Yet, when he was up stairs, he did not feel the least like laughter. The sea lay far and mysterious in the yellow shine. If ever he were back in town he would have a wheeling master, and a golfing, and a swimming ; and he had said he could wheel and swim now. Ah, he must. He would learn the wheel early to-morrow ;

and, remembering, he rang, and told the man to call him at six o'clock. He certainly could do that. As for swimming —he could, a little. To be sure, he had not been in the water for years; but, at least, he could make some sort of an appearance if he did not venture out too far. Of course, he had exaggerated in saying that it was the one thing he could do better than another. He smiled grimly.

"I seem to be getting to be quite a liar; and why?" He answered himself: "She's the most interesting girl I have seen for a long time, I'm sure."

II

Ferguson, the groom, was one of the most observant of his kind; and, being much with his master and mistress, was an accurate measurer of men. From his very walk he could tell whether a man was accustomed to a horse; and, now that wheels had come into his province,

he could put instantly your wheeling gentleman; and, standing there at the stable
door, his arms akimbo around his claret-
colored cheeks, touched with the sunshine,
that brought out a ruddy glow a temperate
but regular attention to the whiskey flask
had given, he decided that this gentleman
in the very new breeches and stockings
was not an old hand. "This's what'll
suit yez, sor," he said, taking one from
the room. He noted that the gentleman
did not mount in the driveway, but went
down into the road.

The air was deliciously soft that morning. The sea had changed its roar to a
murmur. Merton felt the moment inspi-
riting, although a certain derision he had
fancied in Ferguson's manner had piqued
him. " I'll show 'em," he said, now well
out of view of the house. The road
stretched white and level direct into the
land. Not a creature was in sight, and so
he began.

But suddenly this thing of steel and

springs became animated, and refused, like a mustang, and when he was mounted, bucked. Picking himself up, covered with the white dust from the shell road, he tried again, with the same result. Hot and already tired, he kept at it stubbornly. He was not the man to yield at a trifle. But this thing suddenly seemed to have gained extraordinary importance, to be entirely out of the catalogue of mere trifles. A boy in a milk cart stopped and laughed. Several others were summoned by the milk boy, who evidently wished to have his mirth shared. But Merton went on, until finally he had the thing going, but uncertainly. Every time he was a bit more proficient. He found himself wheeling with some ease, and thinking that perhaps he was right in believing that he readily could master the creature. Yet a wagon nearly sent it cavorting. It had a tendency to shy and then to tear directly for an obstacle, leaving its rider dismounted dangerously near a horse's hoofs.

The Mermaid and the Duffer

But he would try again. He had no idea of the passage of time. He was flattering himself that he was progressing at last when he heard the crunching dust behind and Priscilla's voice : —

"You fibbed, Mr. Merton. Now you must come along."

"Yes, do come along, Merton," Tom Brinton cried.

Merton did not dare turn about. His machine shied, and as Priscilla turned hers quickly to avoid him it tore the other way with demoniacal persistence. "Oh," cried Priscilla, "I — "

"I beg pardon," said Merton.

And they were in a heap together in the white dust, and Tom Brinton, thinking Priscilla was hurt, was crying, "You infernal duffer ! "

"Are — you — hurt, Miss Spencer ? " Merton said, extricating himself from the tangle.

"Oh, no; I never am, but my wheel is bent."

The Mermaid and the Duffer

"You see I was right about saying I could not ride very well," Merton exclaimed, despairingly.

"Oh, don't mind," she said, while Tom Brinton brushed the dust from her skirt, and her laughter rippled. "Isn't it ridiculous?"

"Yes, it is," said Tom.

"I'll be hanged if I don't think it serious," said Jack, humbly, "for a man to be such a — a — fool."

"We all have to learn," said Brinton, with that exasperating cackle.

"I wish you were a student in my office," said Jack.

"Luckily, I'm not. But I thought — "

"He does," said Priscilla, decidedly. "Only he's a bit rusty." And then, as if to make amends, she looked up into his eyes. "Don't mind, Mr. Merton, we'll have that swim anyway at six this evening."

"Ferguson," Brinton was shouting, "bring Miss Spencer another machine." Ferguson came down grinning.

The Mermaid and the Duffer

" Oi seed him 's no wheeler," he whispered to Brinton.

Merton at first did not venture to answer Priscilla.

" You must not fail me in that swim."

" I indeed won't," he cried at last. " If there 's one thing I can do it 's swimming." And there speech failed him. Ferguson brought up the new machine. Priscilla mounted with a delightful nod. Brinton threw back a broad, laughing face to the discomfited Merton. He could fancy their remarks. " I must swim or sink," he said. " Here, Ferguson, take this wheel. I 've had enough of it. I 'm going in to breakfast. Now here 's a half dollar. Keep your mouth shut."

" Thank ye, sor," said Ferguson.

III

But if he had given that half dollar to Ferguson, he saw clearly that the best way to face the consequence was with bravado. And so at breakfast he told the story on himself, and laughed the loudest. Our man of the fighting legal world had not entirely lost his tact.

" It was Priscilla, I know," whispered the hostess to her husband. " Oh, that girl ! "

But behind all this show on Jack's part was a firm resolve to retrieve himself by the swim in the evening. He would be very careful, and he felt that his little, boyish skill would return with some interest. In recording this continued aberration on his part, I, too, am inclined to say, " Oh, Priscilla ! " How else can you account for so practical a man suddenly becoming queer; how else than " Priscilla," or woman? He had developed a small opinion of himself, and this was another strange symptom. Tom Brinton's dawdling was of more account than all his achievements put together; and he knew this with fierce envy. All of which proves again the axiom that the trifling and the important are but relative.

The Mermaid and the Duffer

And so the day drew on, and the low sun sent its sheen from the western hills far out over the waves, turning white crests into kaleidoscopes of color. And then they all came down from the house on the cliff, laughing and jesting, my friend indeed holding his own, but appearing a rather puny figure among those athletic ones. And there was not Priscilla, but the mermaid who was part of her, and perhaps the most of her. And her yellow hair and the sea eyes caught the glimmer of the late afternoon, as she dove into a breaker, the others following, and Jack Merton not much behind. Yes, he could swim a bit. He hadn't forgotten. One never entirely forgets that skill. And he felt a certain exhilaration.

And then over the crests some one called to him, an enticing, mocking voice; and there was the very mermaid of the poets pushing before him. What would you, or I, or any man have done but follow? And Merton followed well beyond his depth, that merry voice calling him even deeper. And then the muscles remonstrated, and he knew he could not keep up. Where was that excellent judgment which had carried so well in the struggle among men? Here sillily following a girl, he was sinking. All the world and all his past were framed by the green horizon, and he must die. Still she called. The voice seemed to be a refrain of the sea, like Tennyson's verses.

"What's the matter?" she said.

"Don't mind."

She was approaching with long, powerful strokes.

"Lean on me. There," she said, and as her head rose, "I never shall forgive myself. Stop, and don't mind. They never will know. We are but swimming together. Keep back, Tom, Mr. Merton is but experimenting," she added to Brinton, who called, for they were separated from the others.

"In a moment. Are you tired? Yes,

you are. There. We will touch in a moment."

And they touched, and soon were in the shallows.

"You'd better go in now and take some whiskey. A big drink. It's the best thing."

She turned back to Brinton, who stood beckoning.

"Tom," she said, "don't you dare smile. If you ever so much as whisper it I never will speak to you."

IV

I have represented my friend, good fellow that he is, in such a foolish light that I am glad to say here that he himself told of it, as he had of the bicycle escapade, and that he himself began to laugh. His secret chagrin, however, was none the less deep. I can't remove the charge of foolishness as far as being disturbed by trifles

335

may go. Yet he resolved to face his visit out, to lessen it not a day, but to make no more attempts in unexplored fields. That night he approached Miss Priscilla on the subject, but she was strangely silent, and appeared to avoid him. Yet he hid his discomfiture so well that Mrs. Van Brule confided to her husband that after all she might have been mistaken, and that he was proving an entertaining addition to the house party. But in the night by himself all his provocation cried out. To be saved by a girl! How ridiculous! Could he live it down? And then he remembered that he had not so much as said "thank you." "I don't believe my life appears valuable enough to thank anybody for it," said this disconsolate young man. But he resolved to make amends in the morning, and he found a chance after breakfast.

"I — I hope," said he, "that you don't think that I fail to appreciate the good turn you did me."

The Mermaid and the Duffer

"Oh, don't say anything, please; I was to blame."

"You mean you led me on?"

"Please don't talk about it, Mr. Merton," she cried, with surprising pettishness, and to stop him effectively called to Brinton, "Tom, do come here," which Tom did as obediently as if he were her dog.

As the days dragged on she still avoided him.

One night at dinner he said that he was to leave on the morrow. The hostess said she hoped he would make it a week longer, and now really meant so much. Then he noticed that Priscilla was looking at him keenly. How did he interest her? he asked.

After dinner she called to him:

"Oh, Mr. Merton, do come and walk with me on the beach. No, Tom, you can't come."

Then she fell silent, and they were outside by the talking surf. But he could not talk. She turned suddenly.

The Mermaid and the Duffer

" You — you think me an idiot," she cried violently.

" Why — Miss Spencer — that's what I supposed you thought me."

" Don't be silly," she said. " You are clever and brave and have done things; and you think I only care for these — these people — for trivialities."

" Trivialities seem to me very important lately," he said.

" What do you mean ? " she said, looking across the sea.

" I mean that if all these people are trivialities, including yourself, you are the most important triviality in the world to me — if you insist on that definition."

She turned her eyes from the sea to him, and said not at all shyly, but as you might expect a real mermaid to make such a statement, —

" And do you know I believe you are the most important to me ? "

Now, this was in the moonshine, you know, which is eternally putting unreality

338

on facts, so that inside, where he had her
to himself in a corner, he said, —

"But Tom?"

"Oh, we've just been brought up
together."

"That's all," he said, relieved. "But
I'm such an awful duffer."

"At trivial things," she acknowledged;
and then, in a lower tone, and with a
blush : —

"I want a man who thinks and acts,
and will not be afraid to get drowned —
for me."

"If you entice him beyond his depths?"

"Yes, I want him to be enticed, as you
were."

The Lady of the Road

The Lady of the Road

WE discussed it many times after the weary day was over, and the morrow promised but another as weary. We saw before us vacation, and Arcadia. Tommie said you could find it on a wheel; and finally he persuaded me. My persuasion was complete the third day out. To be sure, we had not yet found Arcadia, but we had the flavor of some good health already, and were hopeful that when we least expected it we should cross the boundary. The road had seized our spirits. We knew already why gypsies persist in their gypsying; why the most entertaining pages in " Wilhelm Meister " and in " Kenelm Chillingly " are those where the heroes take the road " over the hills and far away; " why " Prince

The Lady of the Road

Otto " is the most delightful of Stevenson's stories, and " Walking Tours " the most exquisite of his essays, — although I have not heard that he rode a wheel. We recalled that the real charm of " Pickwick " was in the coaching, and the tooting of horns, and that Dick Turpin was more hero than scamp.

And so feeling fit, and our hearts attuned to simple, natural things, we rode into that bosky wood, which was to be the scene of our first misadventure. The road was smooth and promiseful ; through the branches at our right was the glimmer of a lake, where Tommie said we might loaf comfortably for an hour with our pipes. So we left our steeds by the roadside, and went down by that shore, stretching ourselves out for comfortable contemplation. An hour must have passed, when Tommie gripped my arm.

" Look, Fletcher — there in the road."

I followed his eyes, and saw by our wheels — a bit of sunlight on her face —

The Lady of the Road

a most charming young woman who was
gowned in one of those walking costumes
that are now the most admirable achievement of the dressmaker. She was young,
I say, and blonde; and she was smiling to
herself, and looking our wheels over.
One she raised, and — before we even
fancied it — was in the saddle as easily as
any boy, and tearing around a curve, and
out of our ken.

"Well, I'll be hanged!" said Tommie.

"I hope she'll bring it back," said I.

"Particularly as it's my wheel," said
Tommie. But in the road we could see
no trace of her; she had vanished.

"Get on yours, and catch her," said
Tommie.

"Oh, she'll bring it back. She
was n't — "

"Yes, she was — "

"A gentleman of the road."

"No, a lady — times have changed,"
said Tommie, ruefully. "Well, I'm
after her, Fletch."

The Lady of the Road

And he, too, was around the curve on my wheel, leaving me laughing and mourning. But in five minutes he was back, hot and irritable.

" There are three forks of the road just beyond. How in thunder am I to know which she took ? "

" Try your luck."

" It 's bad enough," said he, " I can't afford another wheel this year."

" I think," said I, " that she 's just playing a trick."

" It 's rather near a theft," said Tommie. " Confound you, it was n't your machine."

" No," said I, lighting a cigarette. " We 'd better walk on. She 's gone; the wheel is — well, perhaps it 's pawned by this time."

" You think you 're funny," quoth Tommie. " Ride on, and I 'll walk."

" No," said I, " we 'll both walk. But she was an infernally pretty — "

" Thief."

The Lady of the Road

" Now, Tommie, you don't know that," said I.

" Well," said he, " have n't I the evidences of my senses ? "

" They sometimes lie," said I. For I saw he was not pleased ; it was n't my wheel, and of course I could philosophize more easily than he. We took the most hopeful turn at the three roads, since our map refused to be explicit ; and presently we came on a rustic in boots.

" Did you see a woman riding a man's wheel ? "

" I swan," said the rustic.

" I should remark," said Tommie, " she stole my wheel."

" You don't say ! " said the rustic.

" Where does this road lead ? "

" Nowheres," said the rustic.

" Don't you live here ? " said Tommie.

" Since I was born, golly," said the rustic.

" Then where the deuce will this road bring us to ? " I asked, impatiently.

The Lady of the Road

" That depends on where ye 're goin'," remarked the rustic, practically.

" Oh, Lord!" said Tommie. " I 've a notion to pound this fool."

The rustic looked frightened, and re-treated a step.

" We want to go anywhere — to find the stolen wheel," said I.

" This 'ere road goes to Arcadia," said the rustic.

A female Dick Turpin! Arcadia! We opened our eyes.

" It 's a queer name that Merivale calls his place," said the rustic. " It 's 'round that thar turn."

We left him, despairful of getting any-thing more lucid from him, but it appeared that at least we had reached Arcadia. I began to laugh, when Tommie said irri-tably, " Shut up."

About the turn we came on a road leading from ours between high gate-posts; and there on a grassy bank was our lady of the road. I stepped back, embarrassed. She was laughing to herself. Yes, she was undeniably pretty. And as we paused, she began to sing in a voice that probably was not a good one, by common standard; but here in the wood, singing to herself, it seemed singularly delightful. I clutched Tommie and held him back.

> " Sing no more ditties, sing no more,
>   Of dumps so dull and heavy,
>   The fraud of men was ever so,
>   Since summer first was leafy."

" And of women," said Tommie, stepping forward, cap in hand; at least he remembered so much of his manners. The singer started, and drew herself up.

" Sir ! " said she, like the affronted lady in the play.

" I beg your pardon," said Tommie. " That was a very pretty song."

" What is that to you, sir ? It's Shakespeare."

" You 'll excuse me," said Tommie;

349

"but we have had a mishap. My wheel has been stolen."

"Stolen!" she cried in a crimson glow; and then in a tone that went despairful: "Down by the lake?"

"Yes, down by the lake," said the malicious Tommie.

"Oh," she cried, "how can I explain? There it is. I thought it was Fred's. I thought Fred and Harry left them there."

"It's no matter," said I. "I'm sorry. It was a natural mistake."

She looked at me with a world of thanks in the blue eyes. Did I tell you before they were blue? Tommie calmly walked to his wheel.

"I am glad you did it," he said, "because it has given me a chance to know you."

"You're atrocious," she said; and turned and fled up the road behind the gateway.

"Tommie," said I, "you're a cad."

The Lady of the Road

Tommie leaned on his wheel, laughed, and whistled.

"Was n't she jolly?" he said. "I 'm going to follow."

"You are not going to do anything of the kind," I cried. But he always is stubborn; and it ended by me following him.

II

The road led from the wood into a broad sunny lawn which was dominated by a great stone house, where a man was just stepping into a high dog-cart.

"Why," said Tommie, "it 's Harry Wharton."

At the moment Wharton saw us. "Well, I declare," he cried, coming forward.

"She did n't lie after all," said Tommie. "He 's the Harry of the 'Fred and Harry' probably."

"Did you think she did?" I cried fiercely; but Tommie was explaining

351

The Lady of the Road

to Wharton that we had lost our way,
and Wharton was insisting on the hospitality of the Merivale house, which he
had rented for the summer, he explained ;
and Tommie was accepting, while I stood
speechless. At the moment our lady of
the road came out of the house and blushed
at the sight of us, and looked as if she
wanted nothing so much as to take to her
heels, which were very pretty heels, I must
assure you, topped by a delicious ankle.
Wharton presented us, " Miss Rose
Burton." Tommie had the audacity to
say, " We 've met before."

" You have ? " said Wharton.

" I don't remember," said she, giving
Tommie a glance that would have
troubled me, but only seemed to delight
him. But she rewarded me by turning
to me, and extending her hand and saying
in a low voice, " I don't see why your
friend is so odious about that mistake."

" I don't know, I 'm sure," I said.
Mrs. Wharton just then appeared, and I

had her — I don't mean Mrs. Wharton —
quite to myself, — an opportunity I tried
to deserve. I began to believe that
Arcadia was all the poets have claimed
for it. I told her that I knew it was
a mistake from the first; and, to be frank,
I did n't try very hard to defend Tommie's
churlishness. I told her she had rather
startled me when I saw her mount
Tommie's wheel like —

" Like a boy," she interposed.

" Oh, I don't know," said I.

" How Harry and Fred — "

" And Fred ? " I said, beginning to
suspect every man.

" Oh, he's my brother. How they'd
laugh, I was going to say. But a joke
is with him who laughs last — with your
friend, I think."

" He thought you Dick Turpin disguised," I said, trying, I 'll confess, to
make his case a bit worse.

" He might have known," she said, as
if much provoked.

" Yes, he might," I assented.

Yet in strict fairness, I felt called on to let him know my perfidy; and that night as we sat smoking and reviewing the day's adventures, I said, —

" She thinks you insufferable, Tommie."

" She has told you that already ? "

" Why, yes," I replied, with rather a self-conscious air.

" I say, Fletch, I believe there 'll be more fun in this house than on the road. I don't believe that we can have another adventure — like — "

" Like getting your wheel stolen. Do you want another ? "

" She 's an amusing girl," said Tommie, inconsequently.

" Yes, she is," I agreed. " But — you see you 've offended her."

" And you have n't ? "

" Oh, I don't know. I said from the first you would get your wheel back — "

" And you told her that ; and that I insisted she was a thief ? "

The Lady of the Road

" Well, yes," I admitted guiltily, " I believe I did."

" And you think she 'll like you any better for running me down ? " he asked as sarcastically as he could.

" Who said I wanted her to like me ? "

" Your manner — you conceited ass."

" You 're the conceited ass, Tommie; for you think you 've made an impression."

" Well, now that you mention it, I hope I may have."

" And that I have n't ? "

" Well, yes," Tommie answered honestly.

" You think you can by being disagreeable ? "

" Look here, Fletch, let 's solve for ourselves that moot question, — which way will make the most impression on a girl like that — flattery or brutal frankness."

" We may break her heart," said I, resolved that of us two, I, not he, should do the breakage.

" I think she 'll look out for that," Tommie said.

" Or she may break ours," I commented.

" We 'll risk that," said Tommie.

" We may end by disliking each other," I went on.

" Oh, if I lose, I 'll not hold it against you," said Tommie.

" But I may against you," I said.

" Such a Tom-boy sort of a girl, too ! " said Tommie.

" I think you wrong her. I have found some fine qualities — "

" Oh, you have ! Well, you 're a quick one," he retorted.

III

Those dear people who formerly lived in Arcadia successfully eliminated pain and jealousy and rivalry — at least judging from their own accounts ; they doubt-

The Lady of the Road

less lied a bit about it. For in my own experience I am bound to say that there may be drawbacks, even to Arcadia. My consciousness of a flaw in the place began when I saw that Tommie was absorbing rather too much of her attention. I felt at first that she was but leading him on, and then I began to have some grave suspicions, which, in the light of subsequent experience, may indeed have been founded on mere jealousy. Yes, I will say I was jealous. I thought in beginning this veracious account that I might well leave the solution ungiven — like the famous riddle of the lady and the tiger. Of our two systems of tactics, which was the more likely to win with a girl like Rose Burton? If Tommie at times had the better, there were other days when I seemed to be more in her favor. Once I accused him of using my flatteries, of not playing fair, when he retorted that I had known him long enough to trust him.

"You never can trust even your best

friend — when there's a woman in the case."

"Fletcher," said Tommie, gravely, at this, "that ancient saying is gospel truth."

From that moment I felt that it was not a fair test case; but indeed I had ended by not caring a fig about the test. I just wanted to win.

Now, one day the climax of the situation was reached in this wise. I heard she had gone wheeling by herself. That, of course, was a chance. I prepared to follow, when who should appear but Tommie.

"Which way?" he asked.

"I was thinking of following, hem — "

"So was I," he said.

"It's ridiculous for us both to follow her," I observed.

"Yes, it is; but I'm not inclined to turn back, for — "

"Nor I," said Tommie, quietly. "It's fair to leave it to the wheels. The one who overtakes her first — "

"All right," I said.

The Lady of the Road

And then began that contest which a certain Tartar tribe conduct more regularly, — a chase for a lady; up and down hill we scorched; now I before — now Tommie. But it was oftener Tommie before than I. He drew away from me; until in sheer spite at my luck and him, I gave it up, dismounted, and wandered drearily enough into the wood and threw myself down; and then fell to laughing, when I heard voices — hers and Tommie's. I declare I could n't avoid hearing them.

"Ah, I have been chasing a thief," he was saying.

"Will you never stop teasing me?" she cried. That remark seemed to show that he had been playing fair after all.

"Will you keep my heart which you stole — "

"That's a very silly speech," she said. I thought so, too. "Besides, it was a wheel," she added.

"No, it was the other essential to a man's comfort."

359 .

The Lady of the Road

"Well, if you'll have it so," she said.

As for me, I turned away. They didn't notice me. In the evening I ventured to say to her, —

"Ah, I've been congratulating Tommie."

"He told you?" she said, turning very red.

"Ah, yes," I fibbed. "You know I thought you thought him — well — rather disagreeable."

"I did — at first. But — you know I believe that was the reason I thought so much about him that — " She paused in confusion.

"Then it's true that you can make more of an impression on a girl by being disagreeable to her than by flattering her."

"Oh, I don't know," she said.

I don't believe she did.

Now don't think that I am still nursing a broken heart. I am too old a bachelor not to know there are many good fish in the sea.

Part IV
A Tale of an India Mystery

The Square Diamond

THE " Britannia" pitched in the Biscayan swell, and the crowd in the smoking-room had lessened until five men were left, exchanging yarns, as men will who go to and fro in ships. Captain Willoughby had been silent through most, and only the subject of Indian trickery seemed to arouse him. Now and then the screw gave its dismal whir, the men drew closer, and the steward hurried with the Scotch, almost tumbling in a quick lurch.

" You know that old trick, when the fakir takes a boy, cuts him into pieces, and then puts him together again ? " said the short fat dark man.

" Yes, but I never knew a man who could swear positively he had seen it."

The Square Diamond

" I have seen it," said the short fat dark man, swigging his Scotch.

" And I," said Captain Willoughby, beating a tattoo with his boot.

" But while we stood at first in horror, in amazement, a boy climbed down a tree, saying he had seen the fakir cut up a squash — that was all," said the short fat dark man.

" You mean that the boy was outside the mesmeric circle ? Do you believe that bosh ? " said one.

" I do," said the short fat dark man.

" I do," said Captain Willoughby, decidedly.

" Oh, you do ? "

" Yes, for I know," said the bronzed captain, who bore his fifty years as lightly as a coquette her second affair. He paused, looking about. Still the screw whirred its chorus to the now beating storm. Willoughby suddenly reached into his waistcoat, taking from a little leathern case a ring, in a curious setting, — a single, square diamond. Holding it up, he asked, " Do you notice that ring ? "

" It's beautiful," said the short fat dark man ; " and the setting an antique, too. But it's hard to sell a square stone, the dealers say."

" Yes," said Willoughby. " But the setting is new, — an imitation ; I had it made for the stone."

" Yes, but what has this to do with occultism and our fakir ? Is it the old tale of the Rajah's diamond ? " said the sceptic.

" Yes, the old tale," said Willoughby, soberly. He put the ring back into its case and looked about. He was not given to story-telling, and yet to-night the whirring screw, the beating storm — some strange impulse — led him on.

" I will tell you how it was," he said, stretching his long legs. " That stone cost me the best servant, and, indeed, the best friend a man ever had, — an Irish boy who was brought up with me. You may say what you will about theosophy, or occultism, or fakirism. I only know what I have experienced, and there are twenty men in the Sixtieth Bengal who will bear me out. I am too old a man, gentlemen, to sneer at the unknown. I have not lived in India, and spent my youth and some health, without having reached the knowledge that the unknown sits in the lap of the known, and that there is some curious relation between matter and mind which doubtless will be made known some day. Only the day before our sailing you heard of the Roentgen discovery of the cathodic rays. Why may there not be some light that one mind may shed on another, creating an illusion? That is mesmerism, you may say. Why may there not be a material object, like my square diamond, which may be able, in connection with some particular personality, to produce certain illusions?"

"Can you do it with your diamond?" asked the sceptic.

"Listen," Willoughby continued, almost

sternly, " and I will tell you why I always carry that stone with me, a circumstance which may appear strange. I don't know why I tell the story now; but I have begun, and something seems to make me.

" Two years ago I had been down in the old place in Devon, and there developed a sentimentality — you know how it may be with a very old bachelor — requiring a ring. Passing a shop in Regent Street, I saw in a tiara — a new one, made in an old fashion — this stone. I have a fancy for unusual things, you know. The man agreed to take the stone from the tiara."

" ' Your taste is excellent, sir,' he was pleased to comment, in their way. ' The stone is very old; five thousand years, maybe; an Indian stone from an old tiara.'

" ' The present setting is modern.'

" ' Yes, I tried to imitate the idea of the old piece — that is all. I came by the stone very curiously.'

" ' How curiously ? '

" He moved uneasily.

The Square Diamond

" ' I can't tell you, sir.'

" I looked at him narrowly; yet it was one of the best shops in London, and why should I ask questions? We bargained a bit, and securing the stone at a remarkably low price — it seemed to me, considering its intrinsic value and Regent Street — I drew myself a design for a fitting setting to carry a unique gem. But when my ring was ready, my sentimental affair was over, like many another in my life; and I simply had the ring, instead of its once probable wearer. On my return to India, and in my duties, which came over me with all the force of habit to a man long in the service, I almost forgot it.

" Well, a year ago, if you may remember, came the little trouble with the little Rajah of Renaub. You may not even remember it, or know that Renaub is on the northern border among the Himalayas. The affair did not amount to much, and I, with some twenty men of the Sixtieth Bengal, had reason to curse it

The Square Diamond

—and particularly my servant, Teddy Burns, had his reason, poor devil!

"In the first place, we were stationed in a narrow, barren, gray valley, a pass perhaps a quarter of a mile broad, with a sheer rise of the gray mountains five thousand feet each side. The valley is about fifteen miles wide, opening at the north on the plateau of Renaub. We were at a wretched village, some five miles from the northern opening, a station with an official. The official had a wife, a pale little London woman, worn out by Indian life. I pitied the pair from the bottom of my heart in that God-forsaken spot — not the only dismal spot in India, as I know. We played cards, and talked, and drank, until we were tired of ourselves; and the man's sad-eyed pale little wife would chatter of London, and tell how she longed to see just Trafalgar Square.

"One afternoon, going back to my quarters, I had occasion to look for something in a box, when out tumbled a case with

The Square Diamond

some pins and trinkets which Teddy had put in, probably thinking that Renaub was a gay spot, and that I might wish to dress up. I opened it, throwing out among other things the ring, which I had forgotten. What I wanted was a little painting on porcelain — very decently done — of our place in Devon, which I wished to show to the homesick woman. As I looked at it, leaving the other things on the table, I heard a rustling behind, and saw a tall, thin native peering over my shoulder. His ascetic face was illuminated by great eyes, with a reddish glow as of rubies — greedy, covetous.

"'What the devil?' I began.

"'Did the Sahib call?' he said, bending. I thought he might be a servant I had not seen.

"'Get out!' I said, simply; for such a place leaves you irritable; when he turned, and, with all the dignity of a personage, stalked through the door.

"'Teddy,' I called, thinking Teddy

372

could not be far away.   And sure enough
Teddy appeared.

"'What are you coming to in your old
age, that you need an assistant to help you
now?' I asked.

"'What d' yez mean, sor?' said Teddy,
most respectfully, although the words may
not so sound.

"'Who was the man in here just
now?'

"'I saw no one, sor.'

"'Did n't you pass him, coming in?'

"'Who, sor?'

"The matter seemed strange.   I knew
Teddy would n't lie; and I concluded it
had been some familiar servant who had
the run of the house, whom, in a short
stay, neither Teddy nor I had noticed.

"'Put those things up then,' I said,
knowing Teddy was incorruptible, and
starting to take the porcelain to our
official's wife.   I hardly was at the outer
door when I heard a scuffle and a muffled
cry.   With a sudden fear I rushed back,

and at the threshold, for a moment, stood horrified. Teddy was stretched speechless in a pool of blood, a knife with a strangely carved handle sticking in his side; and a stealthy figure — the same that had faced me so shortly before — stood over him. For a moment we looked at each other; for a moment I could not move; and then, with a snarl, the creature sprang toward me. I was ready for him, but he slipped through my hands, and passed me — through the door.

"Raising a dreadful cry, I was after. At the outside door I saw him, a lithe figure, that had dropped the loin-cloth from his naked legs, running up the valley, past three of my men, who were on ponies.

"'Stop him!' I cried. But he slipped past; and before they had recovered from their astonishment I was by them.

"'Go in! Look to Teddy,' I called, dragging one from his pony and taking his seat.

The Square Diamond

"'After him!' I said, kicking my brute. 'Shoot him, if you can bring him down.' I had n't my pistols.

"And we chased up that brown valley under the glaring North Indian sun. He seemed to run as fast as our ponies; but at last we gained a little. He looked about, showing white, grinning teeth. Two of the men answered with pistol-shots. I bent well onto the pony's neck.

"'Where is he?' asked one of the men.

"'Where —?' began the other.

"For before our eyes the runner had vanished, faded, what you will; and where he should have been was a lean wolf, turning now and then hungry eyes, and snarling lips, and grinning teeth.

"The thing was so uncanny that I pulled up my pony; and then was charging up to the spot where the man had disappeared and the wolf appeared — believing he had found a hole in the earth. But there the short, yellow furze was unbroken. There was another click and report — a long, horrid, brutish howl — and the wolf was over a low slope, too, out of view, and the men after. After a moment I followed, to find them dismounted by the man we had been chasing — without a wolf in sight; the man on his back.

"'Damn it, sir, where's the wolf?' one of my bewildered fellows asked.

"The great eyes stared brutishly up to mine. One fist was clinched. With sudden expectation I leaned over and opened the sinewy fist, when from it fell the ring. I put it into my pocket, leaving the men with the dead thing, and rode back to Teddy, only to be met by my friend the official. Teddy was dead, like his murderer, who proved to be unknown at the station, and was probably some wandering thief.

"I told the eager listener of our hallucination.

"'The men will swear to it, and I.'

The Square Diamond

"He looked at me a moment, curiously.

"'I have lived too long in India to doubt it,' said he, slowly. 'Tell me how did you come by the stone?' When I had finished he asked, strangely: —

"'Have you not heard that a certain mind associated with a certain talisman can produce such an illusion?'

"'I have seen it,' said I.

"As I said at the beginning of this story, 'I have seen it.' That square diamond at any rate cost me the best servant a man ever had — more than servant, a friend. Whether it were ordinary cupidity, or some desire for that particular stone, I cannot say. But I saw the wolf where the man was, and the dead man where the dead wolf should have been. Some persons would have given the diamond away, or have sold it, but I have kept it."

"There was no boy up a tree outside the mesmeric influence," said the sceptic. "May I see that stone again?"

"Yes, certainly," said Captain Willoughby, taking the diamond from the case. "That thing happened a year ago to-day."

They passed it from hand to hand; and above the storm roared.

"Will you mind if I look at it, sir?" asked a low, distant voice. They looked up startled, for no one had seen this last entering; they saw a tall, dark person, modishly dressed — with all the western affectations of some East Indians.

"You were listening," said Willoughby. "I did n't hear or see you. I must have been so absorbed in my story. Certainly, sir. I should like to have one of your race look at that stone."

A lean, sinewy hand stretched out, grasping the stone. Willoughby shivered and looked up.

"Where the devil?" he began; for hand, and ring, and man, were not there. They rubbed their eyes, ran into the passage.

The steward was called. He knew no

one on the ship answering the description, nor did the thorough search the next morning show the thief; perhaps he had been some strange stowaway, perhaps he had been washed from the deck.

The " Britannia " then was tossing and groaning in the arms of the roaring storm, and, as far as that ship's company was concerned, the dark-visaged unknown seemed to have gone back into the tempest whence he had come.

A Tale of the Ghost
of the Stretching Moor

The House of the Bronze Fox

The House of the Bronze Fox[1]

I HAD had all kinds of predictions of what might happen in that region; but yet exactly nothing had, although an official of one arrondissement had detained us two days. I say us; for, although I had started alone from Genoa for the long eight hundred miles' wheel, I had come, early along the Corniche road, on Pierson, a little chap from Manchester, who was deploring a punctured tire, and whom I helped with my kit. He, too, was in search of the adventure of the road, and fell easily into my purpose, and I had

---

[1] This tale has been reprinted so often, in England and America, without the author's name, or credit to the original publication, that the author has been tempted to add it to this collection.

found him quiet, and not too cleverly distracting. I, indeed, don't know what I should have done without him in the long distances beyond Marseilles, when on the fourth day we fell into a region of peasantry speaking a patois that was about as impenetrably dense as their superstitions and distrust of strangers. Yet, all went well enough until that afternoon, when in a desolate stretch of moor we rode into the jaws of howling thunder and tossing rain. The way fell a bit hilly and rutty, with a coating of sickening mud to retard. Drenched and disheartened, the moor seemed limitless. We must have erred at a cross-road; for the inn we hoped for did not appear: not a house, nor a human being, nor dog nor sheep. We might have turned back, but we had come so far that it seemed better to paddle on with dull persistence. The scurrying wet bit our faces brutishly; and our legs were like mechanical metal cylinders, had it not been for their remonstranceful aching; and, to

The House of the Bronze Fox

add to our weary dismay, the night reached
across the waste, crushing us with fear-
some shadows. We indeed were about
yielding, when suddenly a burst of livid
lightning showed a great battlemented
house to which the path led, — displayed
it surprisingly, for it seemed as if we
should have seen it before. Directly we
were on it, and, leaving the wheels, poked
toward it, wondering why none had given
us question, and why there was no gleam
of light through any chink. A great outer
gate was open, and we groped to an inner
at the bottom of the narrowing passage;
and then a more penetrating flash struck a
glare over a broad door, and there looked
down a great bronze fox's head with the
knocker ring listless from its jaw. Our
impatience left us no discretion; the blackness was provoking; and I raised the ring,
which struck a chill through my gloved
finger. The spot where it fell may have
been cushioned; for we were dumfounded
by silence, when the door was opened as of

its own volition, — sending a certain splen-
did glow over us, — the light of many
candles, and the sight, and strangely not
the crackle, of a burning log in a deep fireplace at a long hall's end. The furnish-
ings, elaborate in the extreme, were of
Henri Quatre. Portraits and mailed figures
lined the walls. The flickering light sought
the polish of the oaken flooring and ceil-
ing; and close at the door was a lackey,
— a tall, dark fellow, with a dash of the
hired bravo you gather from old books and
old pictures ; for he was dressed in livery
fitting the period of all the decoration of
this interior. His voice surprised us quite
as much as this unexpected splendor of
light that no chink had revealed to us
when groping outside; a faint sounding
yet distinct tone, in French that we understood, although it seemed not exactly the
French we were schooled to, no more than
the patois of that district.

" The Sieur de Bellaire, sirs, has been
waiting you, and despairing of your appear-

ance has sat down to dinner, telling me to show you there."

I began, and Pierson bore out my disclaimer, that he was mistaken; that we could not be expected; that we were simply itinerant bicyclists lost in the blindness of the storm on the stretching moor. And we wondered who this gentleman could be who displayed so bizarre a taste in furnishing and in the dress of his lackey, in this forsaken spot; adding this new aberration to many previous ones in my observation of the eccentricity possible in eccentric millionnaires. Surprise was doubled by the man's quick retort:

" Ah, gentlemen, no mistake has been made — I assure you."

And although he looked at us slyly, yet his manner seemed to reflect a master's cordiality. I thought of all I had heard of strange personages who keep their doors open for chance guests. Perhaps a glass had revealed us a-struggling on the moor along the path ending in this unexpected welcome. And, mistake or no, our condition and weariness and hunger, made us accept, after our proper disclaimer had been disallowed. We asked but to go back for our wheels, when the man said he would care for them, and that his master ought not to be kept waiting longer. The master would excuse our appearances, if we should join him at once; and we, now inclined to see the adventure to its end, followed with some amazement that the burning log on the hearth seemed to give out no warmth; and, yet, perhaps the chill from the moor had reached the marrow so penetratingly that a whiff of heat failed to affect us.

We were ushered into a great dining hall where a table was elaborately spread with quaint and strange dishes, — all, it seemed, of the gone day of Henri Quatre; and it was a gentleman of that period, nicely attired in silk and hose and flowing linen, who bowed urbanely, and motioned us to the board where places for two showed that we alone were expected. Yet for a moment we paused, oblivious of manners, at the host's face : thin, narrow, clever, cunning, high-bred, with strange tossing black eyes; and the voice had that same French, which had certain antique phrases reminding me of an *essai* of the Sieur de Montaigne. For the Sieur de Bellaire appeared to have that nice sense in this masquerade which Mr. Irving brings to the setting of a play, where accuracy in every detail is to be sought. The mouth put the expression of this gentleman's face, — with cruel lines and eager white teeth now and again showing, — something belying the graces of exquisite breeding. Yet when he spoke this feeling faded, and we sat, on his motion, to our places.

"You have kept me waiting, gentlemen," said he, with gentle suavity; "and yet I think you will find the dinner not so bad — for a country house."

We again cried out a mistake had been made; when he smilingly said that this was not so, and that were it not for the favor of the storm he should have dined alone. The man who had admitted us returned, and became the waiter, gliding about, serving us, and pouring out from a dusty flagon some heavy wine that sparkled with delicious suggestiveness, and sent a subtle fire which stole the chill away. We began to talk with loosened tongues, while our host watched us as if amused at our subjects; as if he indeed were a gentleman of the old time who heard us as one might the redoubtable Baron Munchausen; watched us with a sneer that was only half covert; and yet, while listening, said absolutely nothing of himself; and but shrugged his shoulders when we exclaimed at the exact taste which had made this perfect illusion of a long gone day. And when we had done — remarking at the oddity of the viands, as well as at their appetizing qualities — he still said naught of himself, leaving us wondering the more at the Sieur de Bellaire; that we never should have heard of him; and that any person, even with a millionnaire's power, could produce such an effect.

" To-morrow," said he, and I fancied a gleam of his eyes and a twitching of his lips, " I will explain. Now, I know you are weary, and Theodor will show you to your lodging, which I hope may prove satisfactory."

When we answered that nothing could be more pleasingly perfect than this choice hospitality to belated strangers, he bowed with sudden, curt dismissal, while the man, candle in hand, beckoned to the door. Not wishing to press our appreciation — in this sudden display of haughtiness —we followed, through interminable corridors, into a great damp, tapestried chamber, where the servant lit a score of candles, that but seemed to increase a sense of gloom. A great bed, such as you may see in the museum of Cluny, was at one side; but the room was singularly cheerless, as the servant's steps sounded and faded out-

The House of the Bronze Fox

side the closed door. Then we turned to question each other's impression; to voice our wonder; to notice a fox on the mountings; to pause with sudden horror and amazement at a full length portrait of our host opposite the bed. There he stood, looking at us in Henri Quatre costume; the same restless eyes, the gleam of white teeth under thin exasperating lips. And watching, I grew to fear and hate that face.

Pierson shared my feeling. The whole adventure had been so unaccountable, the object of our entertainer even on the score of eccentricity so inexplicable, that, as sane and strong as we were, we readily agreed to lie down on the bed without removing our clothes, and to leave the candles burning. A heavy key turned rustily in the lock. When I crept to Pierson's side, he already seemed to be sunken in slumber, as was reasonable after our many weary miles that day. But I at first could not sleep, as exhausted as I was.

The House of the Bronze Fox

That striking portrait faced me and made me dread ; and yet, at last nature had her way.

I waked suddenly with the dread gripping my heart — awoke horribly in the pain of nightmare, my eyes on the portrait of the Sieur de Bellaire, that the still flickering candles showed. Or was it the portrait ? I stared ; I feared. Ah, such horrid fear that it was ! sickening me even now. The Sieur de Bellaire was advancing out of his frame, was nearing me ; and suddenly leaning forward thrust his teeth into my throat. I could feel a stinging, biting pain ; and then I had strength to exert myself against the Thing. We strove mightily : I for life, the Thing for desire. I know of nothing more terrible than that struggle. I know of nothing that sends a chill like that of death through the veins even now. For this was a struggle of life and death ; the thing was ice that froze my heart, that wanted my warm blood to thaw its own iciness of death ; and as we

The House of the Bronze Fox

rolled and struggled, I heard no sound from Pierson. Was he dead? I knew not. And sometimes the cruel Thing with the bestial fangs had the better; and then the desire for my own life was greater than its desire for it; and I mastered it. Yes, life mastered the thing of death that fought for the life in me; and when I knew that I had thrust it from me, my life went out of me.

And yet I don't know. If it had been that I died — that Pierson died — I should not be telling this story. I awoke, with a sense of warmth, among tall grass, and the life-giving sun on my face; and raising myself, I looked out on a far reach of moor, the sun of the day-break caught in the yellow grass tops. No person, no living thing was in view; yes, there was a house on a near road; but where was the battlemented house of the night before? And I saw Pierson sleeping at my side; and then, raising himself, he turned on me a fearful, questioning stare. I noticed our

396

wheels lying at our sides, as if we had fallen from them where we were. And then I had a pain at the throat, and feeling there knew it had been torn, and was still bleeding; and Pierson's throat had some unaccountable mark.

Shortly we began to question each other in hoarse unnatural voices; and his story was as mine. Yet we said nothing in surprise. We did not call each other liars! For we knew. And, so, too lame to mount even when we found the path, we turned toward the house we had seen, limping, with aching muscles.

The house proved to be the inn we had been seeking in the night's storm. There we breakfasted, and then began to ask in the tap-room of the Sieur de Bellaire, of the House of the Bronze Fox. Perhaps they did not understand, for as we questioned they slunk away. But a barefoot mendicant, a brown cowled monk who was listening, came forward crossing himself, and surprising us with excellent English:

The House of the Bronze Fox

" You passed a night in the House of the Bronze Fox ? "

" Yes."

The monk looked at us curiously, again fingering his rosary.

" Who is this Sieur de Bellaire ? "

" There is none."

" There is none ? "

" He died in Henri Quatre's reign."

" He died ?   And the house ? "

" There is only the cellar where the house was."

" And what of that we saw ? "

" Who knows ? "

The monk paused strangely, —

" Have you ever heard that there may be dead who try to steal the life from the living ? " he said with strange, searchful eyes on me ; and he turned, still fingering the rosary, and went out of the door. We paused, looking at each other, and then too late — for the monk had gone — tried to inquire of the men in the inn. They but stared at us stupidly as not understanding us; nor could we make anything of their patois.

Pierson pulled me out into the sunshine, his face ashen, and motioned to our wheels. I understood, and with that same impulse of flight, too, mounted. The sun had dried the mud coating on that good road; the summer morning drove the night out of our brains; and as we wheeled along, our pulses again beating regularly, our blood warm, the events of the night grew dimmer. They seemed but parts of a nightmare. It was as if we both had had a fall in the storm that had left us unconscious until dawn; that had put the same scars on our throats; that had stirred the same fancies in our brains. Nor now can we be positive that it was else than dream — an accident, when in the tempest we wheeled out of our path, and the weariness of utter exhaustion wrought strange delusions. When late that afternoon we were wheeling in a wooded country no one seemed to know even the location of the

The House of the Bronze Fox

moor; nor have we since been able to put it. It was all a nightmarish thing, that may or may not have come from physical exhaustion, we said; and yet, saying so much, we turned on each other eyes of dread lest there might be contradiction; and even yet, it is the same with us on the subject of that dream of the moor.

PRINTED AT THE UNIVERSITY PRESS,
IN   CAMBRIDGE,   MASSACHUSETTS,
FOR STONE AND KIMBALL, PUBLISH-
ERS, NEW YORK, M DCCC XCVII